W9-BJJ-117

"Why not admit you enjoyed being kissed?"

Brent's voice was teasing. "Is it impossible for you to do so?"

"It would depend upon knowing what you hoped to achieve by that brief encounter," Lana replied.

Brent was silent for several moments before he said, "I'm not sure. Perhaps... just a little love, a little kiss. Haven't you ever heard of the word *impulse*?"

"Oh, yes, I've heard of it. You decided that I was there for the taking, so why not take? Wasn't that the situation?"

"Not exactly. You're forgetting that *impulse* also means 'sudden urge or desire'—and it was really the desire to hold you close to me."

Firm fingers beneath her chin turned her face toward him, and while she knew that now was the time to run, it seemed as if she lacked the power to move....

Miriam MacGregor began writing under the tutelage of a renowned military historian, and produced articles, books—fiction and nonfiction—concerning New Zealand's pioneer days, as well as plays for a local drama club. In 1984 she received an award for her contribution to New Zealand's literary field. She now writes romance novels exclusively and derives great pleasure from offering readers escape from everyday life. She and her husband live on a sheep-and-cattle station near the small town of Waipawa.

Books by Miriam MacGregor

HARLEQUIN ROMANCE

2710—BOSS OF BRIGHTLANDS
2733—SPRING AT SEVENOAKS
2794—CALL OF THE MOUNTAIN
2823—WINTER AT WHITECLIFFS
2849—STAIRWAY TO DESTINY
2890—AUTUMN AT AUBREY'S
2931—RIDER OF THE HILLS

Don't miss any of our special offers. Write to us at the following address for information on our newest releases.

Harlequin Reader Service
901 Fuhrmann Blvd., P.O. Box 1397, Buffalo, NY 14240
Canadian address: P.O. Box 603,
Fort Erie, Ont. L2A 5X3

Lord of the Lodge

Miriam MacGregor

Harlequin Books

TORONTO • NEW YORK • LONDON
AMSTERDAM • PARIS • SYDNEY • HAMBURG
STOCKHOLM • ATHENS • TOKYO • MILAN

Original hardcover edition published in 1988
by Mills & Boon Limited

ISBN 0-373-02996-9

Harlequin Romance first edition August 1989

Copyright © 1988 by Miriam MacGregor.
All rights reserved. Except for use in any review, the reproduction or utilization
of this work in whole or in part in any form by any electronic, mechanical or
other means, now known or hereafter invented, including xerography,
photocopying and recording, or in any information storage or retrieval system,
is forbidden without the permission of the publisher, Harlequin Enterprises
Limited, 225 Duncan Mill Road, Don Mills, Ontario, Canada M3B 3K9.

All the characters in this book have no existence outside the imagination of
the author and have no relation whatsoever to anyone bearing the same name
or names. They are not even distantly inspired by any individual known or
unknown to the author, and all incidents are pure invention.

® are Trademarks registered in the United States Patent and Trademark Office
and in other countries.

Printed in U.S.A.

CHAPTER ONE

LANA sat on the upper reaches of the sand where clumps of tall marram grass sheltered her from the light southerly breeze. The muted murmur of a calm sea sang in her ears, while the late afternoon sun washed her bikini-clad form with a delicious warmth. Four miles across the sparkling deep blue water lay Kapiti Island, the soft bushclad face of its six-mile length rising to remind her of the body of a gigantic whale, beached for ever more in this area of the Tasman sea.

The sun's dazzle on the ocean caused her to close her eyes, and as she did so she made an effort to suppress the tremor of excitement swirling about in her mind. She knew that the recent forty-mile drive from Wellington had nothing to do with her inner turmoil, and that her entire nervous state stemmed from her reason for being at this place.

In an effort to calm her nerves she breathed deeply to fill her lungs with the tang of clean sea air, and as she did so she admonished herself mentally. Relax, you fool. Nobody knows who you are or why you're here. All you intend to do is observe, and then slip away quietly. Just satisfy your curiosity and then go home. No harm can be done to anyone and your mind will be at rest—well, at least to a certain extent. But only to a certain extent, she admitted, suddenly conscious of a niggling doubt concerning the wisdom of her actions.

She opened her eyes once more, then blinked against the sun's glare as she saw she was not alone on the beach. A Greek god, or someone very much like one, appeared in the waves rippling along the water's edge, and, blinking again, she knew it was not her imagination. Where had he come from? Had he stepped from the depths, or had the dazzle on the water kept him obscured? And then she realised she had been so deeply engrossed with her thoughts she had failed to notice the lone swimmer in the sea.

She watched as he strode across the beach, then stiffened as she became aware that he was making his way towards her. Moments later he stood before her, his dark hair shining wetly, his athletic form complemented by a handsome face with regular features. She also became conscious of his dark eyes appraising the slim lines exposed by her bikini and finally coming to rest on the mounds of breasts swelling above her bra.

She snatched at her yellow towelling wrap and threw it across her body, a hint of defiance creeping into her blue eyes as she spread it from neck to knee. He had come to her, so let him speak first, she decided, waiting in silence for the sound of his voice. When it came she was struck by its timbre.

'I saw you come down the track from Leisure Lodge,' he said. 'Are you a guest?'

'Yes.' Was he also a guest? she wondered, staring up at him, then dragged her eyes away from the short crisp hairs curling across his broad chest. They were as dark as the hair on his head.

He studied her with interest, his eyes lingering on her face. 'You must have arrived late this afternoon.'

'Yes.' He'd be about thirty-two, she decided, guessing at his age.

'How long do you intend to stay?'

'Only a few days,' she replied politely. Was this any business of his? She lowered her eyes, then found difficulty in keeping them away from the muscled legs placed slightly apart. Wet sand glistened on the dark hairs above his knees.

She followed its line toward his thighs, then shifted her gaze away from his small swimming-briefs.

'A few days should be enough time for trouble,' he informed her in a dry tone of voice.

'*Trouble?*' The word startled her. Surely this man couldn't have guessed who she was or the reason for her visit. No, that was quite impossible. 'What do you mean by trouble?' she asked hesitantly.

'That fair skin of yours, it won't take too much sun, so be warned.' His eyes left her face, then moved to her smooth arms. 'You don't appear to have had much sun this summer. Perhaps you work in an office and the weekends have been poor for sunbathing?' His dark brows turned the words into a question.

Lana gave a rueful sigh. 'I'm afraid so. Fine days in Wellington always come during the week.' She stopped abruptly, annoyed to find herself admitting she came from Wellington. The less people knew about her, the easier her project would be.

He said, 'You'll find the climate along the coast vastly different from Wellington. At this time of the day the sun is past its danger point, but you must remember that February is our hottest month, when the combination of sun and sea air can do much damage to complexions as fair as yours.'

Her smile revealed white, even teeth. 'You're the local protector of the district's blondes?'

'Not exactly, but I dislike seeing visitors leave Leisure Lodge with bodies and faces the colour of ripe tomatoes. I've seen the pain that can be suffered from unwise sunbathing.'

Thank you for your concern.'

'There's one person at the lodge who learnt his lesson the hard way. He has colouring similar to yours and wouldn't dream of going out in the sun without his old straw hat.'

Interest sparked as his words brought a secret smile to her

lips. *Colouring similar to hers.* I'll know him, even without his old straw hat, she thought. Aloud she said politely, 'Are you connected to the lodge in some way? I mean, are you a guest?'

'No, I'm not a guest.' He grinned as though the thought amused him. 'I suppose you could say I do the odd job about the place.'

Puzzled, she said, 'You appear to be rather young for an odd-job man. I've always thought of them as being much older.'

Her remark caused him to laugh, then he said seriously, 'Don't forget to keep yourself well oiled with suntan lotions or whatever.'

She looked down at the towelling jacket that still covered her. 'I can manage my front and arms and legs, but my back defeats me.'

'Then ask somebody to do it for you. I'm usually around the place. I'll oblige, if you'll allow me. It would be a most pleasant—er—odd job. Just ask for Brent.'

Lana expected a grin to accompany the words, but he remained deadly serious. 'Thank you, I'm sure it won't be necessary to bother you,' she said quietly, looking down at the sand. The mere thought of his hands on her back almost made her spinal nerves tingle.

'OK, so don't neglect to use it.' It was an order issued in sharp tones.

Her delicate brows rose as she asked evenly, 'For a stranger, aren't you being rather bossy?'

'Perhaps, but the welfare of guests happens to be one of my jobs.'

'Really? Then I'm sure we're all in good hands.' It was difficult to keep the amusement from her voice. 'Does it mean you spend your time advising people?'

His dark eyes glinted at her. 'Certainly not. However there's one further suggestion I might offer: don't go swimming when the tide is a long way out. There's a strong rip that can carry you under.'

Before she could reply he was striding towards the nearby path leading up to the lodge, and with his departure the emptiness of the beach forced itself upon her. The air took on a sudden coolness as the sun dropped closer to the horizon, its sinking cloaking the island with an eerie gloom.

Lana sprang to her feet, slipped her arms into the yellow jacket and snatched up her beach-bag. The marram grass whipped her bare legs as she ran up the sandy track, and when she crossed the lawns in front of the long veranda she noticed that the umbrellas had been removed from the outdoor tables.

When she reached her room she showered in the small en-suite bathroom attached to the bedroom, and later regarded the clothes she had hung in the wardrobe. The selection was not extensive because she had brought only a few dresses with her, and now she paused to consider her two most recently purchased garments.

Eventually she decided upon a full-skirted dress of deep violet that contrasted with her creamy complexion and pale gold flaxen hair. The neckline was more daring than she was accustomed to wearing, but her pearl necklace and earrings would take some of the bareness away. She knew the dress suited her, and suddenly she felt grateful to the twins for persuading her to buy it. A smile touched her lips as she recalled the way in which they had bullied her into making the purchase.

'Go on, be a devil and buy it,' Raewyn had urged, her brown eyes sparkling.

Lana had demurred. 'Don't you think the neckline's a little low? Look at that *cleavage*! Mother will have a fit.'

Bronwyn's cheeks had dimpled. 'No, she won't. Anyway, so what? You've got beautiful boobs, so why not show them off?'

The saleswoman had giggled. 'She's right, you know.'

'The colour is gorgeous—quite dramatic,' Raewyn had

breathed. 'It makes your eyes go all purplish-blue.'

'It's sophisticated,' Bronwyn had added. 'It's what you need, something to give you oomph and a spot of dash. It stops you from being so pale and—*ethereal.*'

'Isn't *anaemic* the word you're looking for?' Lana had asked drily.

The saleswoman, with an eye to business, had immediately produced another dress of entirely different style. The satiny gold-coloured material had been cut on more subdued lines to feature a mandarin collar, plain sleeveless bodice and fully flared skirt that swung from a lowered hipline.

Lana had hesitated, torn between the two dresses because she considered the gold one to be more versatile, but the twins had decided the question. 'Take both dresses,' they had urged in unison. 'You might meet somebody really dishy in that holiday place.' And then Bronwyn had added, 'You might find a man to sweep you right up into the clouds where you'll need to be really well dressed.'

Raewyn had become scathing. 'Don't be silly, Bron. You don't need to wear *anything* if you're up in the clouds.'

Lana had laughed. 'Are you girls trying to be rid of me, to push me off the shelf?'

But the twins had seen nothing humorous in the question. 'Gosh, Lana, you're *twenty-three*. It sure is *time*. Besides, we're just longing to be bridesmaids,' Raewyn had declared while Bronwyn nodded in agreement.

The saleswoman had then clinched the deal by saying with sincerity, 'Both dresses definitely do something for you, and there's a special discount price.'

Lana had written a cheque for the two garments, and now as she stepped into the violet dress she could almost hear the twins declaring that she would really cut a dash on her first night at Leisure Lodge. Nor did her choice have anything to do with the man she had met on the beach. Of course not. How could it?

Who was he? she wondered as she attended to her make-up. A wine waiter with a little free time before dinner? She could imagine him sitting at a table to drink the wine, but not serving it. Or maybe he was in charge of the horses? The brochure on the table said that Leisure Lodge provided horses for riding along the beach, or over the fields which formed the farm attached to the guest-house. However, her mind's eye saw him galloping across country on a thorough-bred, rather than leading an elderly nag that was suitable for people who did not normally ride.

Could he be the person who organised the bush walks in the Tararua foothills where he would have to make sure that guests did not stray or become lost? She doubted it. He would be away, striding ahead of the party, impatient to reach the depths of the forest.

Thinking about him, Lana found herself unable to fit him into any of the activities advertised by the brochure, mainly because there was a dominance about him, a faint arrogance that obscured all visions of servility. Yet he had declared the welfare of the guests to be one of his odd jobs. Anyone looking less like an odd-job man she had yet to see.

She dragged her thoughts away from him, again focusing them on the twins whom she had always looked upon as her sisters. Actually there was no blood relationship between them, because they were the daughters of her adoptive parents, Eunice and John Glenny, who, being childless at the time, had adopted Lana soon after her birth.

Lana had always known she was an adopted child because Eunice had never made any secret of the fact, and even eight years later, when Eunice had amazed John and herself by producing twins, her affection for Lana had remained constant. 'These are the babies who were *born* to me,' she explained to the little fair-haired girl, 'but you are the one I chose.'

It was only when Lana reached her teens that she began to wonder about her own natural parents, but when she questioned Eunice, her adoptive mother usually became evasive and would tell her very little. However, when Lana had reached the age of fifteen, just as the twins were now, she had begun to question Eunice with more determination, yet still with very little in the way of results.

And now, wandering to the window to gaze at the island rising from the darkening sea, she recalled that particular day when Eunice had said, 'My dear, I've *told* you, your mother died when you were born.'

Lana had looked into the brown eyes. 'Yes, I know she died, but what about my father? I presume he lived.'

Eunice had shifted her plump form uncomforatbly. 'Oh, yes, he lived, but it was his situation and his attitude that enabled us to adopt you.'

The statement had been difficult to digest. 'His *situation*—his *attitude*? Then you do know *something* about him.'

Eunice had gathered her wits. 'Nothing at all, my dear. Haven't I told you repeatedly that all adoptions go through the Government Department of Social Welfare? Their officers must approve the homes the babies go into, and they insist upon strict secrecy so that any relationship with the natural parents is completely destroyed. In this way the child is absorbed into the family of the adoptive parents. Believe me, there have been cases where mothers have tried to contact children who have been adopted. They've made attempts to drag them back, causing situations which have been most upsetting for everyone, especially for the child.'

But Lana was not to be fobbed off with these explanations, most of which she had heard before. She looked at Eunice thoughtfully as she said, 'Mother, if everything is supposed to be so—so very secretive, how do you know my father had an attitude of any sort, or a situation to contend with?'

'It's only what I heard from Rita.'

'Rita? Do you mean Father's cousin who died last year? What could she possibly know?'

'Well, she was a nurse before she retired, and as it happened she was nursing at the home when you were born. She told us about the poor man. When his wife died he was quite beside himself with grief and obviously not capable of thinking straight. It was Rita who really guided you into our hands.'

'And now she's gone,' said Lana. 'It's too late for her to tell me anything about him. Oh, if only I had *known*, if only you'd *told* me.' Her eyes had filled with tears of reproach. 'Didn't she even tell you his name?'

'I'm afraid she couldn't remember it,' Eunice declared evasively. 'As for me, I did what I thought was best.'

'What did she mean by his situation?' Lana had queried.

'Just the fact that he and his wife were alone in New Zealand. Neither of them had any relatives who could take care of a new baby.'

'But his *attitude*?' Lana had persisted. 'What did she mean?'

Eunice had compressed her lips, remaining silent as she looked down at her *petit point*. The fine needlework was developing into a knight on horseback beside a tree and would eventually be framed into a picture to be hung beside numerous others.

Again Lana had appealed to her. 'Are you sure she didn't say anything more? What did she mean by his attitude?'

Eunice had controlled her impatience with an effort. 'Really, dear, I'd rather not talk about it.'

'Why, Mother? Why won't you tell me?'

Time had been taken to rethread a needle. 'Because I don't want you to be hurt. Isn't that reason enough?'

'How could he possibly hurt me at this late date?'

'By knowledge of his attitude towards you at the time or your birth. Really, I *wish* you wouldn't persist.'

But Lana had persisted. 'Please tell me.'

Eunice had sighed, looking at her with troubled eyes. 'Very well, if you insist. The truth of the matter is that he blamed you for your mother's death. Rita said he was so distraught he even refused to look at you. To be blunt, he completely rejected you.'

Lana had looked at her wordlessly. The revelation had come as a shock, causing her to cringe within herself. Her own father had actually rejected her? He had blamed her for her mother's death and therefore he wouldn't even *look* at her? It seemed incredible.

The stricken expression on her face then caused Eunice to say, 'I'm sorry. I shouldn't have told you.'

'But I asked for it, so it isn't your fault.'

Ever practical, Eunice had said, 'Then try to forget it. Be thankful you weren't dumped into an orphanage and that your lucky stars sent Rita to organise you into home life. We're not wealthy, but I doubt that you've wanted for much,' she had added drily.

'You're telling me to count my blessings,' Lana had responded. 'OK, I'll do just that, not forgetting that you've also provided me with a couple of sisters.'

'I wish they looked more like you,' Eunice had said wistfully as she had regarded Lana's clear complexion, her large blue eyes and the pale gold of her flaxen hair. 'Instead, they'll be exactly like me, too plump and too determined to get their own way. Now let's have a cup of tea,' she had added by way of changing the subject.

It had taken several weeks for Lana to get thoughts of her natural father out of her head. During the daytime when she was busily occupied by her job in her adoptive father's accountancy firm it had not been so difficult, but at night, when she lay in bed, the faceless spectre persisted in entering her mind. It was almost as though he was trying to tell her something, and one night she realised the truth.

Of course—it was exactly as Rita had explained to Eunice and John. The man's mind had become unhinged by intense grief, coupled with shock. He hardly knew what he was doing. It meant he had loved his wife very deeply, therefore it was little wonder he couldn't bear to look at the baby he considered had caused her death.

After coming to that conclusion Lana ceased to dwell upon her natural father, although a vague curiosity concerning him continued to lurk in the back of her mind. There were times when questions plagued her. What did he look like? How did he earn his living? Had he married again, and had he completely forgotten her mother and herself? After all it was years ago, and life must go on for everyone.

During the next eight years life went on as usual for Lana. She had been given more responsible work in the office and her salary had risen sufficiently for her to save money to buy a small car. Nevertheless her days were filled with a sameness that even the few parties she attended were unable to enliven. Her life lacked excitement of any sort and she was becoming bored.

In the meantime the twins had almost grown up. They had passed the worst of the twittering stage, although the odd giggle was apt to burst forth. At fifteen they considered themselves to be knowledgeable adults, and this assumption became even more pronounced with the attaining of their driving licences. They became concerned about Lana who had reached the age of twenty-three without being attached to a serious boyfriend, and they began to worry about her sinking into the status of being an old maid.

However, an incident that would bring change for Lana was about to raise its head. It had occurred one evening when John Glenny sat reading his paper, and when Eunice and the girls usually knew better than to disturb him. Slippers on his feet, a glass of Scotch on the small table beside him, his peace was suddenly shattered by Bronwyn leaning over his shoulder to peer at the paper and ask a question.

'Daddy, what's that bit about adult adoptions?'

His voice had come impatiently. 'I don't know. I haven't read it. I doubt that it's anything of interest to us.'

Raewyn had said, 'It's probably something to do with the change in the adoption laws. I'll bet Lana's been following it.' She had sent a sly glance across the room.

Lana had been following it, but she said nothing.

Bronwyn persisted, 'Well, I haven't been following it, so what does it mean? What's all the fuss, and what's to be different?'

'There's no fuss and it's quite simple,' Eunice said quietly. 'It means that the the Adoption Act has been altered. The secrecy has been removed, and children who were adopted when young are now given the opportunity to search for their natural parents.'

John rustled his paper, then said drily, 'I understand that some of the parents are not too happy about it.'

'Why should they be unhappy?' Raewyn's tone was indignant.

He ran a hand over the top of his balding head. 'Because it can cause embarrassment. It can upset entire families or even lead to blackmail.'

'So what can be done to prevent that sort of trouble?' Raewyn pursued, her brown eyes widening at the thought.

'People who have no wish to see a by-blow from the past land on their mat can put a veto against their name in the appropriate government department. It's probably the Department of Social Welfare.'

'People have no right to have babies and then forget about them,' Bronwyn cut in with some heat.

'My dear, it depends upon circumstances,' Eunice told her quietly. 'Not all adopted children are illegitimate, you know.'

Raewyn became thoughtful. 'Does this change in the Act mean that Lana could find her real father?'

'If she feels so inclined,' Eunice said, a cool note creeping into her voice. 'Personally I consider that John had been a very good father to her.' She laid the everlasting needlework in her lap as she turned to Lana. 'Have you ever really wanted for anything?'

Lana shook her head. 'No, of course not.'

'You've been given a good education. You've never had to search for a job, the firm pays you an excellent salary and we've both given you love. Is there anything else we could have given you?'

'Only roots.' Lana had not meant to say the word but somehow it had just slipped out.

They had all stared at her until the silence had been broken by Bronwyn. '*Roots?* What do you mean? You've got *us*, haven't you?'

And Raewyn had echoed, 'I don't understand. Why should you be worrying about roots?'

'She means her own personal background,' John Glenny had tried to explain to the twins.

'It's all behind a closed door,' Lana had said in a small voice 'Can't you understand? You have aunts and uncles, grandparents who are blood relations, but when I look at them I know I don't belong because there is no family resemblance. And when I try to look at my own forebears the door is shut fast.' She looked appealingly from one to the other as she added, 'I'd love to open it.'

'Of course we understand,' John had said kindly.

'So what does this mean?' Eunice's needlework remained idle in her lap as she gazed at Lana. 'Are you saying you want to find this man who deserted you? Do you intend to leave us, after all we've done for you?' Her voice had risen in agitation.

Dismayed, Lana had cried, 'No, no of course not.'

John had spoken sharply. 'Calm yourself, Eunice. You're jumping to conclusions. Why don't you let Lana explain what she has in mind?' He had then turned to peer across the top of his spectacles. 'Now then, Lana, I feel sure you're simmering over a plan of some sort. Why not share it with us?'

She had glanced nervously towards Eunice. 'No. I—I still have to think about it.'

'Haven't you been thinking about it already?' he had pursued shrewdly. 'The pros and cons of this change in the adoption law have been given a fair airing in the newspapers, and now the Act had been passed. I can hardly believe it's escaped your notice.'

'You're right, I have been thinking about it, but please believe me when I say I have no wish to leave you.'

'You'll leave us when you get married, *if* you ever do,' Raewyn had pointed out.

The remark had brought a laugh from Bronwyn. 'At the rate she's going that'll be light years away.'

'Be quiet, girls,' Eunice had snapped. 'Now then, Lana, what would you like to do? Do you intend to go searching for this man?

She had decided to be frank. 'Yes, I'd like to look at him. I'm curious about his appearance. I'd like to talk to him, to learn what type of man he is. That's if I can ever find him, of course.'

'And then what?' Eunice had pursued anxiously.

'And then I'd come home. Life would go on as usual, but I'd feel a little more satisfied within myself.'

'You'd tell him who you are?' the twins had asked almost in one voice.'

Lana had become thoughtful, but at last she had said,

'No. That might cause an upset of some sort because he's most unlikely to want contact with me. He threw me out once so why should he open his arms to me now? At present I just want to look at him, to learn a little about him, and then come home.'

'Then please remember that this place is your home,' Eunice echoed.

Lana then turned to John. 'Where do I begin? Would it be at the Social Welfare Department?'

John had not answered her directly. Instead he had sent Eunice a slightly twisted smile. 'My dear, I think it's time for you to come clean and tell Lana what you know.'

Eunice had sent him an indignant glare. 'Well, *I like that*!' she had exclaimed. 'Time for *me* to come clean indeed! Rita told *you* as well as me, so why am *I* the one to be holding back information?'

Bewildered, Lana had gazed from one to the other while the twins had silenced each other with warning glances. Something was coming up and they had no intention of being sent from the room because this happened to be Lana's private business.

And then John had said to Lana, 'There's no need to go searching through various records. We can tell you where your natural father is living, or at least where he was a couple of years ago.'

Lana's jaw had sagged slightly as she had waited for him to say more.

'Rita told us about him,' he admitted. 'A short time before she died she happened to go into a city restaurant during the busy lunch hour. The place was crowded, making it necessary to share the table with two men and a woman, and she felt positive that the older man was your father.'

'How could she be so sure?' Lana had whispered.

Eunice had broken in, 'It was his hair that had caught her

eye. Don't forget she had seen him before, and his thick,
wavy flaxen hair was something she remembered about
him, coupled with his height and his handsome face.' She
paused thoughtfully, then added, 'I recall Rita saying that
he and his wife had similar hair, and that they could have
been taken for brother and sister. However, he didn't
recognise her, and she just sat and listened to their
conversation. She heard the name Leisure Lodge
mentioned, and from what they said she could tell they
were connected with the place.'

John said, 'It's a guest-house on the Kapiti coast.'

But Lana hardly heard him. She'd had gazed at Eunice
with eyes darkened by reproach. 'You've known about this
since—since before Rita died, yet you never told me.'

Eunice sought for excuses. 'Can't you understand, dear?
We—we didn't want to lose you. We love you and we didn't
want to you to go rushing to this place.'

'Which is exactly what she'll do now,' Raewyn had
chimed in.

'I think it's exciting,' Bronwyn had echoed. 'Please,
Lanie, can Rae and I come too?'

'Certainly not,' Lana had snapped.

'I suppose you'll want time off to go and look for him,'
John had muttered gloomily.

'I believe there's some due to me,' she reminded him.
'Didn't I cut my holiday by half last year when Miss
Watson's father died? I returned to work while she stayed
home with her mother.'

'I seem to remember something about it, he admitted
grudgingly and in a resigned tone. Then, with sudden
vehemence, 'Mind you, I consider you're making a mistake.
I think you'd be wiser to let sleeping dogs lie. Some are not
so friendly when they're aroused.'

But Lana had shaken her head, smiling as she had said,
'This particular shaggy fellow has been on my mind for a

long time. I'd really like to have a look at him. Tomorrow I'll see about rearranging my work with some of the girls in the office.'

And that was when Bronwyn had said, 'You must buy a new dress to wear in the evenings, something really smashing.'

The remark had resulted in the visit to the city shops and the purchase of the gold dress hanging in the wardrobe, as well as the deep violet one she was now wearing.

A glance at her watch told her it was time to go to the dining-room, but as she surveyed herself in the mirror she was assailed by a sudden nervousness. Where, out there along the corridor and down the stairs, would she come face to face with her natural father? Would he be easy to recognise? All she had to go on was a head of hair somewhat similar to her own.

In what manner was he attached to this place? she wondered. Was he the barman, or the cowman, gardener? But more importantly, was he still here? It had to be almost two years since Rita had seen him in the restaurant, and that gave him plenty of time to have left and found work elsewhere. By now he could be on the other side of the world, and in that case her visit would prove to be fruitless.

Well, she was due for a break and a couple of days on the sands wouldn't go amiss, especially if Greek gods were in the habit of stepping out of the water. The image of the bronzed, dark-haired man who had spoken to her on the beach swept into her mind, and she knew that he also must be around somewhere; but although she tried to push him into the background of her mind he continued to loom largely in her thoughts.

She went downstairs to the foyer where she paused to look through the open front door. Coloured lights now illuminated the tables on the lawn, giving the place a holiday atmosphere, and from beyond the edge of marram grass came the sound of the sea.

A girl standing behind the desk spoke to her. 'The dining-room is along that passage. It's just past the lounge.'

'Thank you.' Lana smiled at her, then added affably, 'It's a lovely evening out there.'

The girl's tone became glum. 'Is it? Maybe it is for some, but I haven't noticed anything to send me up in the air.'

'Oh? Something is wrong?' Then, as the girl made no reply, Lana went towards the dining-room.

On entering the well-filled room she remained near the desk waiting to be led to an unoccupied table. A wine-waiter stood nearby, but he was definitely not the man from the beach, and then she noticed a waitress crossing the room towards her.

Plump and with a smiling face, she said, 'You're Miss Glenny?'

'Yes, I'm in room ten.'

'Mr Tremaine would like you to join him at his table.'

Lana was puzzled. 'Mr Tremaine? Who is he?'

The girl's smile became broader. 'He's the boss. He owns this place. I'll take you to his table.'

Lana was lost for words, but followed the waitress to a table in the far corner of the room. The man who rose to his feet at their approach was dressed in a well-cut pale grey suit and a crisp white shirt that seemed to emphasise the suntan of his handsome features. Nor did she have any difficulty in recognising the man from the beach.

CHAPTER TWO

LANA blinked at him, feeling slightly dazed by the unexpected manner in which she had found herself at his table. For several moments she could only gaze at the dark eyes beneath their heavy brows, at the straight nose and at the well-shaped mouth with his hint of sensuousness. She then became aware that she was being studied carefully, his eyes scanning her features before coming to rest on the low neckline of her dress. *Cleavage*, she thought, feeling suddenly embarrassed, then met his gaze with defiance.

'You've arranged to meet a friend at this place?' he asked as though the question held a subtle meaning.

She shook her heads, thankful it was impossible for him to know her reason for being at Leisure Lodge.

His eyes flicked to her ringless fingers. 'But surely you're—attached in some way?' His tone remained casual as he filled her glass with red wine.

'Does everyone have to be attached?'

'Most of the women who come here are definitely attached, either to husbands or to a fiancé. They seldom come alone. That's why I wondered if you were expecting someone to arrive.'

'Why are you interested in these small details?' she parried.

'It's merely the interest of mine host towards a guest,' he assured her. 'If you're alone you could become bored, and that's bad for the place. Do you ride?'

'No, I'm afraid not.'

'Well, there are other activities. This is not a guest-house in the normal sense of the word. It's really a farm holiday

23

place where city people can see a little of country life.'

'I've read the brochure, but to be honest I'll be quite happy to do little more than relax for a few days.'

'You have a job in Wellington?'

'Yes, I work at the Glenny accountancy firm.'

'Ah, yes, you've sighed the register as Lana Glenny. Does this mean you're the boss's daughter?'

'I suppose you could say so,' she replied guardedly. 'Indoor work, you understand, therefore I'll be keen to just laze out of doors, perhaps under one of those big umbrellas.'

'One can laze around anywhere,' he pointed out. 'Here we do things, even to taking walks in the bush, although that means driving a few miles to get there.'

She sent him a level glance. 'I didn't come here to be organised into bush walks, fascinating as they prbably are.'

Unperturbed he went on, 'We have a launch for making trips to Kapiti Island, weather permitting of course. Naturally, we'd never dream of going out in a rough sea.'

'I should hope not.' Lana opened the menu lying beside her.

He said, 'I've already ordered the chef's special for you. Tonight it's toheroa soup, then venison followed by pavlova and strawberries.'

High-handed and domineering, she thought, but smiled as she said, 'Suppose I'm a vegetarian?'

'Then we'll change the order. No trouble at all.'

Conversation then waned as the meal was served, and as she finished the last mouthful she became aware that he had been observing her closely. Feeling that something was expected of her she remarked. 'You have a very good chef.' Then the words died on her lips as a thought struck her. Was her father the *chef*? 'The sea air must have made me hungry,' she finished weakly.

'I trust you'll find more than good food in this place,'

he said quietly, his eyes holding an intangible expression.

'Yes, I'm sure I shall,' she agreed hastily, her mind veering away from any innuendoes that might be lurking behind his words.

She also noticed that his eyes had barely ceased their thoughtful observation of her face, almost as if trying to penetrate her mind, and then their gaze locked as his dark eyes held hers. Her cheeks began to feel warm, causing her to rebuke herself mentally. Watch it, stupid, you're not here to enjoy a short sharp affair with this devastating man, you're here to observe your father—wherever he happens to be.

The remembrance of her father had barely passed through her mind before she realised that Brent's attention had been diverted from her to people who had just entered the dining-room. They were behind her and she did not turn round to see who had caught his interest, but instinct told her they were drawing near, and a few moments later she knew that a couple had seated themselves at the next table.

Brent's manner towards them was one of familiarity. Grinning in a friendly manner, he said breezily, 'Everything is under control?'

The woman's voice said, 'I'm not sure. I'm afraid that trouble might be looming at the desk.'

Brent did not ask for details. Instead he said, 'Were you at the desk when Miss Glenny arrived? She hasn't yet given me permission, but I intend to call her Lana.' He then made the introduction. 'This is Eric and Hilary Halversen. They manage the place for me.'

Lana turned in her seat to look at the couple. The woman appeared to be in her mid-forties, her hair auburn, her eyes hazel. She wore a smart dress of dark green which enhanced her slim figure. But it was the man who caught and held her real interest.

He had risen to his feet at the introduction and was above average height. His fair complexion had become rugged through exposure to sun and sea air, but his most arresting feature was his hair which was thick, wavy and as flaxen as her own. The sight of it made Lana catch her breath, and it was only by an effort of control that she prevented a sharp exclamation from escaping her lips. She was face to face with her natural father; she knew it without a shadow of doubt.

Her gaze became fixed upon the man, the shock of the encounter causing an inner trembling that made her turn pale. She felt unable to drag her eyes from his face, and she feared that if she didn't take a firm grip on herself she would blurt out something idiotic like 'So *you're the man who deserted me when I was a baby.*'

Gathering her wits, she realised it was just the un-expectedness of the meeting that had thrown her off balance. In some vague way she had hoped to be able to observe him from a discreet distance, before any com-munication could take place, and now it was only with the greatest difficulty that she forced herself to look away from him.

She also sensed that the sight of her had had an effect upon him. She noticed his jolt of surprise and saw a bewildered expression creep into his blue eyes as they rested upon her features. However, it disappeared in a flash as he sent her an affable nod to acknowledge the introduction.

It was Brent's deep voice that brought her back to normal. Speaking to Hilary, he said. 'You mentioned something about desk trouble.'

'It's Peggy,' she complained. 'She's asking for her holidays, and at this time of the year when we're so busy.'

Brent frowned. 'Are they due?'

'I'm afraid they'd somewhat overdue. She started with us

twelve months ago last November, but she didn't want to take her holiday then. She asked for it to be delayed until February, even though I warned her it might not be convenient,' she added with an air of grievance.

'Peggy seems to be a reasonable girl,' Brent remarked mildly.

'Oh, she's reasonable,' Hilary admitted. 'The main trouble lies with her sister's wedding. It's taking place away down in Bluff and Peggy is to be her bridesmaid.'

'Has the fact only just come to light?' Brent asked.

Hilary looked guilty. 'No, she told me about it some time ago, but I'm afraid I'd forgotten about it. She's been expecting me to find a stand-in for when she's away.'

Eric Halversen's sandy brows drew together. 'Perhaps she'd agree to take only part of her holiday, long enough to cover the wedding.'

Hilary gave a rueful sigh. 'I've already suggested that, but she's digging her toes in, pointing out that there'll be numerous jobs for her to attend to, and I can see she's determined to be there to do them.'

Eric shrugged. 'I dare say we'll manage somehow.'

'You mean *I'll* have to manage,' Hilary retorted crossly.

His smile was disarming. 'My dear, I'll do my part. I'll spend more time at the desk. I'll combine it with doing the accounts, answering correspondence and everything else I have on my plate.'

Hilary turned to Lana, politely drawing her into the conversation. 'There's more to the desk job than meets the eye. Somebody has to be there to answer the phone, and I have too many other jobs on hand to spend my entire time there. I have to check that the bedrooms are being done thoroughly, and I must keep account of the linen. I must confer with the chef about the meals——'

'My wife is a very responsible person,' Eric told Lana.

'But I slipped up on Peggy's holiday,' Hilary lamented.

'I'm afraid I've been thoroughly stupid.'

Brent's eye's were upon Lana as he said, 'This domestic problem must be quite boring for a guest.'

She turned to him quickly. 'Not at all. I—I was merely wondering if I could help you.'

'You were?' Interested flickered in his eyes.

She nodded. The discussion had enabled her to make a veiled observation of Eric Halversen, and she realised that a few days at the desk would give her the opportunity to talk to him. Forcing a casual note into her voice she said, 'I have three weeks on my hands, if it's of any use to you.'

Hilary turned to her eagerly. 'Are you offering to do the desk job? Do you think you could manage it?'

Brent cut in, 'Lana works in the Glenny accountancy firm. She'll do it with one hand tied behind her back, I'd say.'

She sent him a fleeting smile. 'Thank you for the vote of confidence.' Then, as his gaze continued to hold hers, she became conscious that her heart was beating at a faster pace. The desk job would also enable her to see more of this attractive man, she realised.

'We'll make sure you don't regret it,' he said.

'And we'll be most grateful for your help,' Hilary assured her.

'I'll second that,' Eric added, his blue eyes again regarding Lana's face with interest. 'Tell me, is this your first visit to Leisure Lodge? I've a strong feeling we've met before.'

Her heart gave a lurch as she brushed away the suggestion. 'We haven't met before, I feel sure. Nor are you a man who would be easily forgotten,' she added, thinking of Rita, who had recognised him after so many years.

Hilary said briskly, 'I know I've never seen Lana before she arrived this afternoon.' She turned to her. 'Now then, my dear, let me tell you about the guest-house activities and what working at the desk entails.'

Lana tried to concentrate, but her mind was in a whirl. Her natural father sat within a few feet of her, and this was a fact she found almost impossible to believe. At the same time she knew that in some strange way his presence was being overshadowed by the knowledge that Brent Tremaine's eyes continued to regard her with interest.

She also knew that Brent's attention to her appearance was bringing a faint flush to her cheeks, and she wondered if he would seek her company when the meal was over. However, it seemed as if this hope was to be little more than wishful thinking, because Hilary led her to the foyer where she continued to tell her about the work at the desk.

Eventually the older woman said, 'I'm sure you'll pick it up quickly by spending tomorrow at the desk with Peggy. And now I suppose you feel weary and would like to go to bed.'

But Lana had no wish for sleep, and, leaving Hilary, she wandered out to the veranda where she stood pondering the situation into which a few impulsive words had placed her.

And then she caught her breath as Brent emerged from the beach track. He crossed the lawn beneath the coloured lights, and as he came up the steps she spoke to him. 'Have you been strolling on the sands?'

He walked along the veranda to stand beside her. 'Yes. It's one of my habits when I need to think.'

'You have a problem?'

'At the moment it's a puzzle rather than a problem.' He paused, placing his hand on the veranda balustrade. 'Please understand that I appreciate your offer of assistance.'

'Please, think nothing of it,' she replied casually.

'Surely you understand that it means a lot to us. However, I must admit I'm surprised by your gesture.'

Her brows rose. 'Surprised? This is what's puzzled you?'

'Yes. It seems odd that you should ruin your holiday

because of our problem.'

'You consider I'm stopping work to carry bricks, as the saying goes.'

'Exactly. And I can't help wondering why.'

Lana remained silent, searching for words that would give him a reason for her action.

'You said you had three weeks on your hands,' he pursued. 'You must have had plans for them.'

'Not really,' she admitted vaguely.

'But you're sacrificing your holiday,' he pointed out. 'To me it seems to be quite silly, yet I don't believe you're stupid, Lana.'

'And so you've been churning it over in your mind?'

He nodded without speaking.

Grasping at a straw she said, 'Perhaps I should explain that I prefer to remain settled in one place, rather than to wander aimlessly.' It was a pathetic reason, she realised, but it would have to suffice.

'Then let's hope you'll be happy in this place.' His voice was earnest as he took her hand and brushed it across his lips before leaving her to go inside.

She remained on the veranda for several minutes before going up to her room, and when she crawled into bed she told herself it had been quite a day. Lying in the darkness she could now see the face of her father, but strangely it kept switching to become the image of Brent Tremaine.

Next morning Lana woke refreshed after a night of dreamless slumber, aware that she would be spending the day at the reception desk with Peggy. She sprang out of bed eagerly, and after showering in the en-suite she considered her wardrobe with care. The dress she chose was one she often wore to the office, a deep blue cut on tailored lines.

Peggy told her all she could about the job. The short dark-haired girl looked at Lana and spoke earnestly. 'Gosh, am I glad you're willing to stand in for me. It'll make things so much easier for the Halversens.'

Lana sympathised with the girl's situation. 'It would be a pity if you missed your sister's wedding.'

Peggy gave a short laugh. 'Miss it? You've got to be joking. I've no intention of missing it. I'll be my sister's bridesmaid if it costs me my job, nor do I intend to arrive at Bluff five minutes before she's due to walk up the aisle.'

'No, of course not.'

'I want to be there in time to make sure my dress is right, and to do all the things a bridesmaid is supposed to do. I told Mrs Halversen about it ages ago,' Peggy added in an aggrieved tone.

Halversen. The name rolled round in Lana's mind, gathering itself into a ball of questions. She was really Lana Halversen, although it was impossible to attach the name to herself.

Peggy said, 'There's more to this job than just booking people in or out of rooms. You mustn't forget to write down the names of people who hire small boats. You must note the time they leave and make sure they get back safely. If they're not back within a reasonable time Brent must be told. He's very particular about these matters, nor will he allow children out in small boats without their parents. As for the launch, he usually works that himself.' She paused to send a knowing glance towards Lana. 'Don't you think he's Mr Stunning, someone to make you look again?'

'Is he? I hadn't noticed,' Lana lied.

'You're half blind?' Peggy's voice echoed pity.

Lana smiled. 'Of course not. Well—yes—I suppose he is something to write home about, but I dare say he's well and truly occupied—emotionally.'

Peggy shrugged. 'If he is, it's a dead secret. Several female friends used to drop in, but that was before Camille returned.'

'Camille? Who's she?'

'You'll learn in good time. Now then, the same rules apply when the horses are taken for riding along the beach or over the farm.'

'I'll remember.' *Who was Camille?* Lana wondered again.

'And make sure that guests return their room keys before leaving. You'll find it all quite easy, but if anything bothers you there's usually somebody in the office to sort it out—either Eric or Brent.'

'Brent spends time in the office?' The question came casually.

'Of course. He attends to the farm accounts and to the financial side of the entire place. Eric is mainly concerned with the guest-house accounts. Their paperwork is done between other activities.'

'What sort of other activities?' Lana asked, hoping she would see more of Eric. *Or was it Brent?* No, of course it wasn't Brent. She was here to observe her father, wasn't she?

Peggy went on, 'This morning Eric said something about having to check the wine stocks.'

'And Brent?' Lana asked despite herself.

'He's taken a fishing party out towards the island. See if you can pick them up through the binoculars.' Peggy took a pair from beneath the desk.

Lana carried them to the front entrance where she focused on the island. The blue bush-clad hills and valleys sprang into closer view, and then, near the rocky shoreline, the white dot of the launch could be seen.

'They'll be there for hours and hours,' Peggy told her. 'We'll not see much of Brent today.'

'Oh.' She was conscious of disappointment as she returned the binoculars and moved to look in the office which lay behind the desk. It was dominated by two leather-topped tables, one holding a typewriter, while against the walls were several filing-cabinets. And apart from a large calendar the only wall decorations were two oil paintings of sailing-ships, their canvas billowing against blue skies as they rode white-crested waves.

For the rest of the day she listened carefully and took notes of all that had to be done, and when Peggy left next morning Lana found herself in charge of the desk. But because she knew that Eric and Brent were sitting at their respective tables in the office behind her, she did not really feel she was doing anything constructive until the phone rang.

'Leisure Lodge guest-house,' her modulated voice told the caller, then, listening, she consulted the register. 'A double room for a week from the fifteenth of March? Is it possible you'd like the honeymoon suite? Very well, I'll reserve it for you. Your name, please. Thank you.' She replaced the receiver and wrote in the book.

'Nicely done.' Brent's deep voice spoke from behind her.

She swung round to face him and was immediately conscious of her quickening pulses. 'It wasn't difficult,' she managed to say calmly.

'Even Peg forgets to ask if they'd like the honeymoon suite. I wondered if you knew about it.'

'Peggy told me about it,' Lana assured him, defending the absent girl, 'but I haven't had time to see it yet.'

'Then it's time you did, otherwise somebody might ask for a description and you'd be unable to supply it.' He spoke over his shoulder to Eric, then led her away from the desk and up the stairs.

At the end of the upper passage a door opened into a large well appointed room with a private balcony, windows that gave seaward views towards Kapiti, and over a countryside that stretched to the foothills of the Tararua ranges.

'It's all fairly new,' Brent told her. 'Facilities are here for making tea or coffee and toast, or they can call room service.

A fridge keeps their drinks cool, and the bedroom and ensuite are through that archway.' He crossed the room to stand beside her at the window. 'Would you like your bridegroom to bring you here?'

She could almost feel his eyes watching her intently, and she knew a flush had risen to her cheeks. Without looking at him she said, 'It's all most attractive. The blue and gold gives it an almost royal touch.'

'That doesn't answer my question.' His hand on her shoulder turned her to face him as he stepped closer.

Looking up into his handsome features, she could only nod dumbly as her heart gave a sudden lurch.

And then his arms went about her, drawing her to him as he said, 'I like to think of newly married couples standing at this window to gaze beyond the south end of Kapiti. At certain times the mountains of the South Island can be seen quite clearly.' His hand pressed her head against his shoulder as he added, 'Can you imagine a bride and groom standing here, like this? I'm sure he'd kiss her.'

His head bent swiftly as his lips found hers in a gentle but teasing kiss that was without passion or pressure, but which sent tingling sensations along every fibre of her nerves. And while she told herself she should move away from him she was held to the spot by the spell that caused her eyes to close and her lips to part.

Her response caused his kiss to deepen and brought strength to the clasp of his arms as they gathered her closer to his body, but as she became aware of his leaping desire common sense caused her to push gently against his chest. A shaky laugh escaped her as she said, 'That was quite a demonstration, but how can you be so sure about their actions?'

'Because it's what I myself would do,' he returned quietly. 'And then I'd sweep my bride into my arms and carry her to the bed.'

His words had hardly registered before an unexpected movement lifted her from her feet to be cradled in his arms, and as he gazed down into her face she could only gape at him wordlessly. A few swift strides carried her across the room and through the archway and as he laid her on the bed a strange expression sprang into his eyes.

She came out of her trance in a flash, springing from the bed with an indignant gasp. 'This is too much! I can guess what the average bridegroom's next move would be, but I've no intention of waiting to see what you have in mind,' she flashed at him, then fled from the room, rushing along the passage and down the stairs.

She was breathless when she reached the desk, and for several moments she sat on the high stool, leaning over its polished surface. No doubt he had imagined her to be an easy mark, no doubt the violet dress with its low neckline had given him that impression. Seething inwardly, Lana whipped herself into a fury, but somehow the memory of his lips on hers, caused her anger to dwindle and evaporate.

The ringing of the phone caused her to gain full control of herself, and when she lifted the receiver she heard Bronwyn's voice asking to speak to Miss Glenny. 'Yes, I'm here. Is that you, Bron?'

'Gosh, what are you doing answering the phone?' the younger girl asked with surprise.

Lana ignored the question. 'Why are you phoning? There's nothing wrong, I hope? Shouldn't you be at college?'

'No. It's a free morning for us and everything's the same as usual. Nothing ever happens. Rae and I were wondering how you're getting on. *Have you see him yet?*'

'Yes, of course.' She knew Bronwyn meant Eric Halversen.

'Have you spoken to him? *What's he like?*'

Lana became cross. 'If you imagine I intend to discuss

this matter over the phone you're very mistaken. It's far too soon to tell you anything.' She fell silent as she heard a whispered conversation at the other end.

And then Raewyn's voice came over the line. 'Don't be mean, Lana. Can't you tell us anything? We're dying to know all about him!'

Lana smiled as she imagined the curious pair standing beside the phone in the hall at home. 'I can at least give you a message for Dad,' she said. 'Please tell him I might take an extra week, because the desk receptionist has gone for her holiday and I'm taking her place.'

'Gosh, you're a quick worker!' Raewyn exclaimed.

'Just give him that message. OK?'

'We'll tell him. But Lana, *we want to know—*'

'Goodbye. Don't forget to tell Dad.' She replaced the receiver before more questions could be hammered at her, and as she did so she became aware that Eric Halversen stood watching her from the office door, his sandy brows raised in question.

'I presume it was a call from home.'

She nodded. 'My twins sisters were anxious to know about something. I'm glad they rang because I was able to pass on the message about staying here for longer than I'd intended.'

He remained in the doorway, regarding her in silence, until she was forced to say, 'Is something wrong?'

He shook his head. 'No. It's just that you remind me quite vividly of someone I knew years ago. She had your pale gold hair.'

She forced a smile. 'The world is full of blondes. Isn't it said we all have a double somewhere?'

'It's the first time I've come across this particular double. Your eyes are also similar to hers.' He strode closer to the desk to stare into Lana's deep blue eyes.

Lana returned his gaze unflinchingly. At least he

remembers my mother's appearance, she thought.

At that moment Hilary came into the foyer. She paused to watch them, then spoke sharply to Eric. 'I trust I'm not interrupting anything.'

Eric's tone remained casual. 'No, my dear, I'm merely taking a closer look at the colour of Lana's eyes. She reminds me of—of someone. It's quite uncanny.'

'I suppose you mean Ingrid.' Irritation tinged the remark, but before it could be followed up Hilary brushed the subject aside by saying, 'The next time we're in Wellington I must visit the warehouse. We're running short of towels.' She turned to Lana and said briskly, 'If you see people taking guest-house towels to the beach, please let me know.'

Lana nodded absently, her mind turning over Eric's words and the two small points she had learned. The first, her mother had looked rather like her, which wasn't really surprising. The second, her name had been Ingrid. The door that had opened a tiny crack when she had met Eric had now been pushed an inch further.

Brent came down the stairs a short time later, and by then Eric had returned to the inner office while Hilary had disappeared towards the kitchen. The dark eyes became sombre as they regarded her. 'You're still here? I made sure you'd be half-way to Wellington by now.'

'I said I'd stand in for Peggy, didn't I?' She returned his gaze expectantly. At least he could say he was sorry for having had the temerity to place her on a bed.

Almost as if he read her thoughts his mouth twisted slightly. 'If you're waiting for me to apologise you can forget it. I had a strong impulse to see you on the bed, and so I put you there.' He moved closer to stare down into her upturned face. 'But I'll admit this, I don't know what the devil got into me.'

'It seems clear enough to me,' she told him coldly. 'Didn't you jump to the conclusion that I'm easy; a piece of cake, to put it bluntly?' She turned away, hoping he would not see the misery she felt, and again she decided it was the cleavage-revealing violet dress that had given him the wrong impression.

'You're in the habit of leaping to conclusions?' he asked drily.

'Only when the situation is more than obvious,' she retorted.

'Did you imagine you were about to be raped?' he asked as though quietly amused by the suggestion. 'I can assure you that nothing was further from my mind. After all, you had only to yell to bring the staff running.'

'Then why——?'

'Why did I carry you to the bed? I told you, I had this strong impulse to see you there. I can only think it was because you responded to my kiss. Or is that something you deny?'

Lana flushed as she recalled her response to his kiss and could find nothing to say.

He went on, 'I can only presume you have no wish for the episode to be repeated.'

Snatching at her dignity, she said, 'Is that a promise?'

'If you wish me to make such a promise I shall do so,' he said gravely.

Lana searched her mind for an answer. She had no wish for Brent to promise he would not kiss her again, but she was unable to bring herself to say so. And then Eric's voice came from the office door.

'Who's making promises?' he asked. 'Don't forget that promises are made to be broken.'

The remark lessened the tension, causing Brent to grin as his eyes swept over Lana's slim form. 'So they are. I'd quite forgotten that small fact.'

Eric went on, 'There's a problem with one of these accounts, Brent. Perhaps we can sort it out together.'

They disappeared into the office, the murmur of their voices coming to Lana as they discussed whatever needed to be discussed. And as she listened to Brent's deep tones their recent conversation spun round in her mind, while the trend of her thoughts left her slightly bewildered. She was here to gain knowledge about Eric Halversen and her own background, wasn't she? Then why was she more interested in Brent Tremaine who had no place in her personal history? And why was she glad that Eric had intervened before Brent could promise he would never kiss her again?

A short time later the voices ceased and she saw Brent leave the office, but although he passed the desk he sent no glance in her direction. He's forgotten I even exist, she realised, becoming aware of an engulfing depression, then wondered why the knowledge bothered her.

Nor did she sit with him at dinner that evening, and despite her mental denials she was bitterly disappointed to be waylaid by Betty when she entered the dining-room.

'Mr Tremaine has a guest,' the waitress whispered. 'I'll put you at another table.'

Lana looked across the room to where Brent sat with a woman whose sophistication could never be in doubt. Red hair was dressed in a modern style and from where she stood Lana could see a dazzling smile being sent across the table towards Brent. 'Who is she, Betty?' she asked in a low voice.

'She's Mrs Boyd. Camille, they call her.'

Camille. Peggy had mentioned Camille, Lana recalled, then found herself unable to resist the question. 'Is she somebody very special to Mr Tremaine?'

Betty shrugged. 'You can bet your life she'd like to be. I understand she's someone he's known for years—before she became Mrs Boyd, in fact. But now she's a widow, with plenty of the folding stuff you put in your wallet. If I took you to their table she'd probably stick a fork into you, or at least make your meal miserable,' she added ominously.

'I've no wish to go to their table,' Lana declared coolly, then stared at the menu with unseeing eyes.

Betty became brisk. 'OK, if you can't make up your mind I'll bring you the chef's special.'

When the meal was brought to the table Lana ate without sending a single glance across the room, telling herself she couldn't care less about the woman at Brent's table. In any case she was here to learn about her father, not to become involved with somebody else. Nor did she linger over the meal, and when she left the dining-room she found Hilary at the desk. 'Have you had your meal?' she asked the older woman.

Hilary shook her head wearily. 'No. Eric has just gone in, but I thought I'd hold the fort for a while.'

'Please go in with him. I'll stay at the desk.'

Hilary accepted the offer gratefully, and Lana seated herself on the high stool where she busied herself with several small tasks. All the rooms were full apart from the honeymoon suite, and as she recalled being placed on the bed her cheeks felt hot; although she tried to recapture a sense of indignation she was unable to rid her mind of the feel of Brent's lips on hers, or the clasp of his arms about her body as they had stood at the window.

The heightened colour had barely left her face when Brent and the woman with whom he had dined came into the foyer, and Lana was then able to look more closely at this person known as Camille. It was impossible to be unimpressed by the red hair that gleamed beneath the foyer lights, and then she became aware that green eyes were regarding her with surprise.

'Peggy has left Leisure Lodge?' Camille asked.

'No.' Brent's tone became casual as he introduced them. 'Lana Glenny, Camille Boyd. Peg's gone to her sister's wedding and Lana is merely standing in for her.'

Merely being the operative word, Lana thought crossly. It meant being of no importance and was obviously the rating she held in his mind. Not that it mattered, of course. And then she was startled by Camille's next words.

'Brent, dear,' she almost purred, 'I'm so interested to hear about this new honeymoon suite. How clever of Hilary to think of setting it up. Please show it to me. Or is it occupied?'

'No, it's unoccupied at the moment.' His eyes darkened aggressively as they met and held Lana's gaze. Then, almost as though he read the resentment in her thoughts, his face became cold while returning her angry glare. However, he made no comment as he took Camille's arm and led her towards the stairs.

CHAPTER THREE

LANA turned away. She had no wish to see Brent and Camille ascend the stairs together, yet her mind's eye watched them walk along the passage and enter the suite where she continued to visualise the scene. No doubt Camille would show polite interest in the modern appointments, and then she would stand at the window with Brent. Together they would gaze across the moonlit sea towards Kapiti. Would he kiss her? Would he draw her gently towards the bed?

The thought made her go hot with resentment until she shook herself mentally. Snap out of it, you fool. You don't know any of these things for sure, she chided herself in silence, yet it seemed impossible to keep her thoughts from the suite, the vision of Camille on the bed being all too clear. As for Brent's reaction—he was a man, wasn't he? He wouldn't just *sit* on the edge of the bed. A deep sigh escaped her as the memory of her own closeness to his body caused a strange inner stirring somewhere near the region of her stomach.

Eventually it was Hilary's voice that brought her back to reality. 'Thank you, Lana, now off you go. Peggy always had time off in the evening and you must do the same.' The words held a brisk command.

But Lana had no wish to leave the desk, at least not yet. Brent and Camille were still upstairs and she was plagued by the necessity to know how long they would remain in the honeymoon suite. 'I don't mind staying here,' she assured Hilary.

'Nonsense. You've been at the desk all day. Go out to the

veranda and breathe in some fresh sea air. The evening's beautifully warm and we get so few of them without wind.'

'Perhaps fresh air is what I need,' Lana agreed, recalling her previous confused thoughts, and, leaving the desk, she went out to the veranda. Shouts of laughter floating faintly across the lawn told her that guests were splashing in the moonlit waves of the high tide, and although there were other guests in the garden she was overwhelmed by loneliness.

Turning to stare at the lighted windows of the guest-house, she noticed that the honeymoon suite appeared to be in darkness. Did it mean that Brent and Camille had left the suite, or were they still there in a gloom broken only by bars of moonlight? The thought gave her an unexpected pain, but several minutes later it vanished when she saw them emerge on to the lawn from a side path.

Camille, teetering slightly on high heels, clung to Brent's arm. Nor did she make any attempt to conceal her irritation when he drew her across the lawn towards Lana.

'I meant to ask you if all the horses had been checked in,' he said, his face unsmiling.

'Yes, only two went out today. The stableman reported their return late this afternoon. I marked the book.'

'I told you they'd be all right,' Camille declared pettishly. 'But oh, no, you had to go out to check that all the saddles were back in the stable.'

Lana was unable to resist a remark to Brent. 'I didn't see you come down the stairs. I felt sure you must be still in the honeymoon suite,' she added smoothly.

'*Honeymoon suite,*' Camille cut in, her tone aggrieved. 'I haven't even seen the place yet. I'd hardly stepped in the door when Brent started on about the horses, and the next instant I was being hustled down the back stairs to count saddles in that smelly old stable.'

'It's necessary to keep a check on such matters,' Brent

pointed out. 'One doesn't wait till midnight to learn that guests who went riding haven't returned.'

Lana said, 'If the horses hadn't been returned I'd have told you a long time ago.' She looked at him thoughtfully, wondering if the saddles had been an excuse to leave a place made distasteful by the memory of recent events concerning herself. But this was something she would never know, she realised, watching him accompany Camille to where her expensive sports car was parked near the front entrance.

Nor was she interested, she tried to assure herself, and without waiting to learn if Brent would now seek her company she went inside and up the stairs. She would go to bed, and he needn't think she was loitering about waiting for him. But even before she had reached the top of the stairs she was regretting her decision, and, coming down slowly, she went out to the veranda again.

His tall figure was easy to discern beneath the coloured lights, and she stood watching as he moved among the guests on the front lawn. His pleasing personality became evident as he chatted amicably in his role of the perfect host, therefore she was surprised when he mounted the steps to speak to her.

'Don't be afraid to circulate among the guests, Lana. I'd be grateful if you'd chat for a while to that newly arrived American couple. See if you can make them feel at home by offering a little friendship.'

'The American couple?' Her eyes searched the guests.

'Elmer and Claramae Crosby. They're strangers in a strange land, you understand.' He took her arm and drew her down the steps. 'You don't mind doing this for me?'

'No, of course not.' She was vitally conscious of the feel of his hand on her bare flesh as he led her to where two people sat at the end table.

As the introductions were made the woman beamed at Lana, then began chatting at once while the husband was allowed to put in a word here and there. And as she listened to Claramae Crosby, Lana watched Brent continue to talk to other guests. Later, as she mounted the stairs again, a sigh of disappointment escaped her. How could she have imagined he would have time to spare for *her*?

And this appeared to be the situation during the next few days when she saw little of him, despite the fact that she watched for him to come down the stairs, to walk in the front entrance, to appear before her in the dining-room.

At last, frustrated, she made an attempt to get him out of her mind, and to do this she concentrated upon learning all she could about Eric Halversen. After all, this man who was her father was her reason for being here, yet in some strange way her priorities seemed to have switched from Eric to Brent.

It was during this period that Eric called her into the office. 'Can you use a typewriter?' he demanded hopefully.

The question surprised her. 'Of course. It's something I've been doing for years. Don't forget I'm from an accountant's office.'

He drew a breath of relief. 'Good. I've a pile of letters to be typed. Peggy usually does them for me, and since her departure I've been struggling with them.'

'I'll get to work on them,' she assured him cheerfully, glad of something that would take her mind away from Brent. But before sitting down at the typewriter she moved towards one of the paintings on the wall, peering to decipher the name of the sailing-vessel.

'That's the *Hovding*,' he said. 'The other ship is the *Ballarat*. The *Hovding* brought my Scandinavian forebears to this country while Ingrid's people came on the *Ballarat*.'

'Scandinavian?' Surprise tinged her voice.

'Norwegian.'

'And Ingrid? Who was she?' She almost held her breath as she awaited confirmation of her earlier guess.

'She was my first wife. She died at the time of the birth of our first child.' There was suppressed pain in his tone.

'What happened? I mean, why did she die?'

'Apparently she had a bad heart condition. She'd been warned that giving birth could prove too much of a strain, but she was determined to have a baby.'

'You knew about her heart condition?'

'Not until it was too late. But Ingrid had made up her mind and couldn't be swayed from the idea. She was sure she'd come through the ordeal with flying colours. However, she didn't.'

Lana was afraid to look at him as she asked, 'What happened to the baby?'

'I don't know. Nor, at that time, did I want to know. The child had caused Ingrid's death and I was unable to forgive it.'

Lana felt a surge of anger against him. Her lips tightened as she said, 'I see. Apparently the baby had asked to be born, therefore it was the little one's fault?'

'In Ingrid's mind a baby was definitely asking to be born.' Eric shook his head as though still bewildered by what had happened twenty-three years ago. 'When it was over I was almost raving mad from grief. I couldn't believe Ingrid had died——'

'And so you blamed the child. You made it suffer——' *Careful, careful,* watch your stupid tongue, she warned herself.

He became annoyed. 'What makes you suggest it suffered? The adoption was arranged through one of the women in the maternity hospital, apart from going through all the proper channels. I was assured it was going to a good home.'

'Did you ever try to find that home?'

'Certainly not. The strict secrecy of the adoption law forbade me to do so. I'm afraid you don't understand the situation,' Eric went on impatiently. 'Ingrid had no relatives still living on this side of the world, and my own relatives had moved to live across the Tasman in Australia. So tell me, what was I to do with a new baby?'

'Couldn't you have employed somebody?'

'Definitely not. Nor did I have any intention of even looking at a child who would have been a constant reminder of Ingrid.'

Lana was shocked. 'You didn't want to remember her?'

He gave an exasperated sigh. 'I mean she'd have been a constant reminder of my loss. She'd be sure to look like Ingrid.'

'The baby was a girl?' she asked innocently.

'Yes, a girl,' he echoed wearily. 'Now would you please be good enough to get on with those blasted letters?'

She sat at the typewriter feeling shaken. Her fingers trembled and the papers rustled as she began to examine the letters. Tears blurred her eyes and she knew she had been a fool to pursue the subject which, no matter how much thought she gave to it, concerned a situation that could never be altered.

Eric's voice cut int her thoughts. 'Are you having difficulty in reading that handwriting? You've been staring at it for a couple of minutes.'

She bliked rapidly. 'No, I can read it.'

'You're still thinking about that baby,' he accused her. 'Believe me, adoption was the best thing that could have happened to it, because I was in no state to have the little one near me.'

'Perhaps you're right,' Lana admitted reluctantly. 'Yes, I can see that the child was better off with a couple who would be parents to her.' And suddenly she was overwhelmed by a rush of gratitude towards Eunice and John Glenny who had been so good, so generous to her. Had she appreciated them sufficiently? She doubted it, and was consumed by guilt that sent more tears to her eyes.

This time they did not go unobserved by Eric who watched her dab at them with a wisp of handkerchief. He left his seat at the table and moved to place a comforting arm about her shoulders. 'You're taking this matter too much to heart. It all happened years ago and that baby, wherever she is, will now be a young woman, perhaps with a baby of her own.'

'You find it easy to brush her off with bouts of wishful thinking?'

His tone became curt. 'What do you expect me to do? Whip myself into a frenzy of worry over what became of the child?'

'I'm being a fool,' she sniffed, mopping the last damp traces.

'Don't be ashamed of your tears. They show you to be a sweet, sympathetic girl.'

His arm tightened about her shoulder while he pressed an unexpected kiss upon her brow, but as he did so Brent's voice, stinging with sarcasm, hit their ears.

'Now here's a touching scene! Watch it, Eric, or Hilary will have your guts for garters.'

Lana was appalled. She turned to gape at Brent as she tried to find words. 'It's nothing. He was just—just——'

Brent sent her a mirthless grin. 'I'm not blind. I could see exactly what he was doing. He was kissing you. And if Hilary had come in the doorway instead of me he'd have found himself being served as mincemeat on the plates tonight.'

Eric began to protest. 'You're making too much out of nothing. Lana was upset and I was merely offering a grain of comfort.'

'Why should she be upset?' Brent demanded, his eyes moving from one to the other.

'It's a long story that's better avoided, particularly as I

want those letters typed,' said Eric, directing a pointed reminder at Lana. As he spoke the bell on the reception desk rang and he left the office to answer it.

Brent moved to sit on the edge of the table. He looked down at Lana, his dark eyes holding an expression she was unable to fathom until he spoke in a low voice that simmered with accusation. 'You wouldn't have been making a pass at him, I suppose?'

She was indignant. 'A *pass*? What do you mean?'

'You know what I mean. I suspect you've been encouraging him. You've been looking at him with those come-hither eyes.'

'Don't be ridiculous.'

'But I have noticed your eyes following him.'

It was impossible to miss the scorn in his voice. 'You're raving,' she said defiantly. 'He's old enough to be my—my father.'

'He's only in his late forties, and certainly not too old to be flattered by the attentions of an attractive blonde.'

'You're quite mistaken,' she snapped angrily. 'Now then, would you be good enough to let me get on with these letters?'

'Perhaps you prefer older men,' he pursued relentlessly. 'I can't help wondering—if it had been Eric instead of me who'd carried you to the honeymoon bed——'

Lana glared at him furiously as she hissed, 'You wonder if my reaction would have been different? *How dare you?*' Her eyes became moist again, causing her to dab at them furiously with hands that shook.

Watching her, he said, 'I think we'd better have a talk.'

'Oh? About what, may I ask?'

'About the people who are connected to this place.'

'I can't see that it's necessary, especially at the moment when I must get these letters typed.'

'It can wait,' he said drily.

Lana turned to concentrate on the letters, and as she did so she became aware that Eric had returned to his seat at the table, while Brent had moved to one of the filing-cabinets. She knew vaguely that he was searching for papers, and it was almost a relief when he left the room carrying a folder of them.

She typed rapidly until the letters were finished, and as she drew the final sheet from the typewriter her thoughts returned to her own background. So, she was of Norwegian descent. No wonder she was so blonde. A smile touched her lips as she realised the door had been pushed open a little further. Could she give it another slight shove? In an effort to do so she turned to Eric and indicated the painting of the *Hovding.* 'What made those people come to New Zealand?'

'You mean the Scandinavians?' Are they still on your mind?' His blue eyes regarded her curiously.

'Yes. I know so little about those particular early settlers.' And then her mind jumped to another question, one closer to herself. Hesitatingly she asked, 'Why was Ingrid so very much alone? You said she was without relatives.'

Eric frowned as though not wishing to pursue the subject, but he said, 'She was an only child. Her parents had parted and had left for overseas as soon as their divorce had been made absolute. Ingrid was brought up by her only grandparents in New Zealand, and by the time she married the old couple had died. Now then, I'll sign those letters.'

A short time later Lana was back at the reception desk, answering the phone, chatting politely to guests or dealing with various queries. There were brief moments when memory of the scorn in Brent's eyes returned to niggle at her, but she brushed it aside, feeling grateful to have sufficient work to keep herself occupied. At the same time she felt an urge to explain the situation to him, but this was something she found herself unable to do.

Hilary came to relieve her at five o'clock. 'You've been

indoors all day,' she declared. 'You should go for a swim. There are good waves out there, that's if you like being buffeted.'

'I'll see what it looks like,' Lana said. She left the desk and went upstairs to put on her swimsuit, then slipped into her yellow towelling wrap. But when she reached the shore she decided against a swim in favour of jogging along the beach, so she set off at a sedate trot.

The northerly wind that blew her hair also whipped the waves, causing the expanse of sea between the mainland and Kapiti's long hump to become dotted with whitecaps, while to her right stretched the North Island's Tararua ranges, their tops shrouded in clouds. Breathing in the fresh sea breezes, she had not gone far before she became aware of two horses coming along the beach towards her, and as they drew near she realised they were being ridden by Elmer and Claramae Crosby who were extending their stay at Leisure Lodge.

Lana had now chatted with them on several occasions, discovering Elmer to be a quiet man with little to say, perhaps because he had formed the habit of allowing his wife to speak for both of them. Nor was it difficult for Claramae to reveal her mind. She was a small woman with sharp eyes, and what she said was usually to the point.

And now as they met she drew rein and looked down at Lana. 'Hi there, perhaps you can help me. The Maori names in this country are so difficult they defeat me. I've been trying to remember where there's a special Maori church. Is it at Wai—Wai—'

'Waikanae? No, it's at Otaki.'

'I told you so,' said Elmer with quiet satisfaction. He stared across the sea then asked in a slow drawl, 'Is there any chance of getting to that hunk of land over there?'

Lana said, 'It's a bird sanctuary, and permission to land must be granted by the ranger. Brent could probably arrange it for you, and he could also take you on a fishing-trip.'

Claramae said, 'That fine-looking fellow is certainly impressive. I'm told he owns the whole outfit, the guest-house and the farm that goes with it. Say, are you out to catch him?'

Lana stared at the woman speechlessly. The words had horrified her. 'I beg your pardon?' she said coldly.

'Don't get me wrong. I mean are you trying to catch up with him? We saw you running along the beach so we presumed you knew he's just ahead of you.' Claramae twisted to look over her shoulder. 'All you need to do is stand and wait, because he's on his way back.'

Lana had been standing with her back to the wind, but now she turned and stared at the figure coming towards them. It was Brent wearing shorts and a green T-shirt, and the sight of him caused her to be gripped by indecision. Should she go forward, or retrace her steps?

Claramae picked up her reins. 'Let's go, Elmer. These two young people won't want us around.'

Lana made up her mind. 'I'm coming back too,' she declared.

'See you later,' Elmer said affably as a dig of his heels sent the horse trotting along the sands.

Lana began to follow them, now jogging at a swifter pace with the wind at her back. She heard Brent's voice carried on the wind as he called to her, but she ignored it.

'Hi, wait for me.' Again the voice came from behind her, and again she ignored it, pretending she hadn't heard.

'*Lana, wait!*' The words held a command which caused her to quicken her steps until suddenly there was a pounding beside her and she felt her arm gripped by an iron hand that swung her round to face him. 'Why the hell are you running away?' he gritted.

'I am not running away,' she gasped breathlessly.

'Oh, no?' He glared at her. 'I dare say you'd have slowed down right smartly if Eric had been trying to catch up with you.'

'Don't be stupid,' she snapped in a fury.

His mouth twisted into a grim line. 'Are you sure I'm being stupid? I told you I'd noticed your eyes following him, to say nothing of the fact that I've also noticed his eyes following you.'

The wind blew her hair across her face. She brushed it away impatiently, longing to tell him the truth, but caution silenced her.

Brent said, 'Come up to the shelter of the sandhills. It's time we had that talk I mentioned earlier.'

Lana hesitated, conscious of a sudden apprehension. 'It's time I was getting back.'

He moved closer to stare down into her face. 'Are you coming, or do I have to carry you out of this wind?'

'Very well.' She spoke with reluctance but followed obediently while he led the way to a valley lying between two marram-grass-covered slopes where it was a relief to be out of the wind. The sun was now low in the sky and it was necessary to turn away from the dazzle of its rays.

As they sat on the sand his voice became terse. 'Is it possible for you to understand that I don't want either Hilary or Eric upset? They've both had their share of troubles and are now happily matched. I will not allow the wiles of a charming young blonde to come between them. Is that clear?I'

'*Wiles?* You're being insulting,' she exclaimed angrily.

'What other word is there for it?'

Frustrated, she said earnestly, 'Please believe me, I have no intention of coming between them. My interest in Eric is not what you think.' Too late she realised her last words had been unwise.

Brent jumped on them. 'Ah, so you do have an interest in

him. What is it exactly?'

'I'm afraid I'm unable to tell you about it.'

'Why not?' His eyes were full of questions.

'Because—because it's my own personal business.'

He sighed wearily. 'Let me assure you there's more to this problem than you realise. Hilary is a jealous woman, and if she becomes upset the entire running of the lodge will be affected. Surely you can see that simple fact.'

'Of course I can see it,' she retorted, irritated by his assumption of her lack of intelligence. 'I can only repeat that I have no wish to upset her.'

'Heaven knows I had enough trouble to persuade her to come out to New Zealand and run the place,' he admitted gloomily.

'Do you mean she didn't want to do the job for you?'

'That's right. She was really looking for a different type of life. She and her husband had managed a place for my Uncle John. It was in England—in Cornwall to be exact.'

'Hilary and Eric?'

'No. Hilary and her first husband. Unfortunately he was drowned in a boating accident off the Cornish coast. She then found it necessary to leave my uncle's employment, first because the job called for a married couple, and secondly because she wanted to get away from the place because the sight of foam crashing over rocks at the bottom of cliffs got on her nerves.'

Lana's imagination caused sympathy to swell in her mind. 'I can understand it,' she said softly.

'Can you? I wonder. Have you ever experienced loss by death?'

'Only—indirectly,' she said in a low voice, staring down at the sand, at the same time realising it had been a very direct loss.

'Well, Hilary got a job in a London hotel, and it was when attending a convention of some sort that she met

Eric.'

'He was doing hotel work?' Her interest intense, it was difficult to make the question sound casual.

'Yes. At that time he'd spent about ten years in England learning hotel management until he'd reached the type of job he wanted. He'd lost his wife before coming to England, so they had something in common. Hilary was the first woman he'd looked at since then.'

'Yet he gave up his job to come to New Zealand.'

'That was mainly due to Uncle John's powers of persuasion. Perhaps I should explain that my father had two brothers, the other being Uncle James who was a bachelor. When he went to visit Uncle John he was so impressed by the guest-house he decided to set one up for himself in New Zealand, except that he was going a step further by having a farm attached to it.'

'He knew about farming?'

'Not a darned thing. Nor did he live long enough to try his hand at it, and because he'd taken on too much without knowing the first thing about guest-houses, the place became run down.'

'But he tried,' Lana pointed out gently.

'Yes, the poor old boy, he tried. Uncle John came out for the funeral, and when he discovered that the whole outfit had been left to me, at that time another ignoramus, he declared I needed a first-class couple who would run it efficiently. He also declared he knew the very people for the job.'

'He had Eric and Hilary in mind?'

'Yes. When he returned to England I went with him, and together we went to see Hilary with whom he'd never lost touch. At first she was apprehensive about moving to a new land that was so far away from all her friends, but Eric was keen to have another look at New Zealand,'

'And so they came,' Lana murmured.

'Yes. They've been at Leisure Lodge for eight years.'
Brent turned to face her. 'I'm sure you'll understand my
concern. I've no wish to see the matrimonial applecart
overturned.'

'You're worrying needlessly.'

'Am I? I wonder.' His eyes narrowed thoughtfully as he
regarded her. 'I suppose if I had any sense I'd send you
packing before harm is done. Down the road, as the saying
goes.'

She glared at him angrily, then began to scramble to her
feet. '*Down the road.* Huh, you can save yourself the trouble
of telling me to get down the road. I'll go the moment I'm
packed.'

The dark eyes glinted up at her. 'So—you'd leave Hilary
in the lurch, without help at the desk?'

'Wouldn't it be safer for all concerned?' she lashed at him
scathingly. 'Especially for the smooth running of your
precious guest-house. And let me tell you that the thought
of Eric being in danger of seduction from my wiles is just
too ludicrous for words.'

'Why is it so stupid? You're a very beautiful girl and he's
a man. Besides, you're forgetting I saw him kissing you.'

'You're giving too much importance to that silly incident
because you don't know what led up to it.'

'Then suppose you sit down again and give me a few
details.'

Lana hesitated, then sat beside him again as she said, 'He
was telling me about his first wife who died when their
baby was born. The story upset me and I shed a few tears.
He was merely being consoling.'

Brent stared at her incredulously. 'Are you saying that
Eric actually told you about Ingrid? It's unbelievable.'

Her voice became cold. 'Are you suggesting I'm lying?
How would I know about it unless he'd told me?'

'How indeed? But let me tell you it's been a taboo subject

for years, ever since there was a row over a photograph of Ingrid.'

'Ah, there's a photograph?' She tried to keep the eagerness from her voice as she added, 'I'd like to see a photo of Ingrid.'

'I'm afraid you're several years too late. He destroyed the only one he had soon after they arrived here.'

'Oh.' She fell silent, fearing that anything she uttered would betray her intense disappointment, but at last she felt compelled to ask, 'Why did he do that?'

'Because Hilary demanded it. They hadn't been here very long before Eric took a drive into the Hutt Valley to look at the house where he and Ingrid had lived. He should have gone alone, but unwisely he took Hilary with him. I suppose he expected her to understand his feelings and to respect his memories.'

'But she didn't? She became jealous?' Lana asked with a sudden understanding for how Hilary might feel.

'Correct. That evening she discovered him looking at the only photo he'd kept. Her jealousy bubbled up and splashed over him. They had an awful row during which she pointed out that they were starting a new phase of their lives and she didn't intend to have it ruined by a ghost from his past. She then gave him an ultimatum. Either he destroyed the photo, or she would return to England, alone.'

Lana was shocked. 'She'd really leave him, because of a photo?'

Brent gave a slight shrug. 'Who can tell? At least she remained, so you can be sure the photo was never produced again.'

Lana trickled sand through her fingers, her mind on the photograph. Had Eric actually destroyed it, or had he kept it hidden away in some secret place? A desperate longing to see it began to gnaw at her, but she brushed it aside as

Brent's voice came urgently.

'Perhaps the story of that little incident will help you to realise it would be unwise to have a closer relationship with Eric.'

The word startled her. *Relationship?* She glared at him as she became impatient. 'Can't you understand that he wasn't really kissing me? It was nothing more than a sympathetic brushing of his lips on my forehead because there were tears in my eyes. Nobody could imagine a kiss out of that vague caress.'

'It wasn't like the kiss you were given in the honeymoon suite?' he asked softly, his eyes full of mockery.

A flush stole into her cheeks. 'No, of course not. Surely you could see that much for yourself.'

'There could have been more kisses before I arrived,' he pointed out.

'Well, there weren't. And let me tell you that the honeymoon suite was a rare occasion for me. Even the twins would agree.'

'The twins? Who are they?'

'My fifteen-year-old sisters. Now that I'm twenty-three Raewyn and Bronwyn have me firmly stuck on the shelf among other elderly spinsters.'

The laugh that escaped him transformed his face. 'Tell me about home,' he urged unexpectedly.

'Home? It seems a world away.' His interest surprised her but she lay back against the slope of the sandhill and stared at the sky as she thought of the house in Wellington. Then, without mentioning the matter of her adoption, she told him about Eunice and her tapestry pictures worked with such meticulous care. And as she spoke of the short plump woman her eyes misted while her appreciation of her adoptive mother almost became an ache. In future she would never fail to let Eunice know how much she loved her, Lana vowed silently.

Engrossed in her description of home, she did not notice his change of position until he leaned over her, his eyes holding a sombre expression as they examined her features, resting upon her brow, her cheeks, then lingering upon her lips. And then she felt his fingers gently stroking the line of her jaw, pausing beneath her chin before searching for a vulnerable nerve in her neck.

His voice came teasingly. 'Why not admit you enjoyed being kissed in the honeymoon suite? Is it impossible for you to do so?'

'It would depend upon knowing what you hoped to achieve by that brief encounter,' she replied, watching the play of a muscle near the corner of his lips, and again she realised it was a sensuous mouth. It was perilously near her own, so she turned away to gaze up at a pink and gold-tipped cloud floating against the blue.

Brent was silent for several moments before he said, 'I'm not sure. Perhaps—just a little love, a little kiss.'

She became thoughtful while still staring up at the cloud which was rapidly turning to a deeper shade of rose. 'Are you sure that's all you had in mind? Are you sure you didn't think I'd oblige, just like that? A snap of your fingers was to put me exactly where you wanted me.'

'No, it wasn't like that at all. Haven't you ever heard of the word "impulse"?'

'Oh, yes, I've heard of it. Closely related to the word *whim*, isn't it? And whim can mean a capricious notion, something that lacks real importance. You decided that I was there for the taking, so why not take? Wasn't that the situation?'

'Not exactly. You're forgetting that impulse also means a sudden urge or desire, and it was really the latter that had bitten me—the desire to hold you close to me.'

Firm fingers beneath her chin turned her face towards him, and while she knew that now was the time to spring to her feet and run, it seemed as if she lacked the power to move. Instead, she continued to lie on the sand, her lips tremulous as though waiting to be kissed.

His mouth came down to nibble gently at hers, moving slowly from side to side as though brushing away the inhibitions he sensed to be there until at last he paused briefly to murmur, 'You need to be awakened—lifted up from that bed of ice.'

His mouth returned, tenderly calling for response until his kiss deepened and she felt the stirrings that caused her lips to part. Her pulses raced as the blood begun to pound through her veins, and a tremor passed through her as he gathered her closer to the length of his body.

How or when her arms crept up to his shoulders, then found their way about his neck, she would have been unable to tell, but suddenly she was clinging to him while she gave herself up to the ecstasy of being lifted to where that pink cloud still floated against the blue. She knew that his lips had begun to explore her face, pressing upon her closed lids with the utmost gentleness before trailing from her temples to her jaw, and perhaps it was the softness of his touch that made her relax.

'Ah, that's more like it. His deep voice came huskily as his lips slid down towards her throat, then glided further to the neckline of her towelling wrap. Pushing it aside his eyes reflected an inner fire as they rested upon the rounded swellings of breasts rising above the bra of her swimsuit, and with a sigh he buried his face against their cleavage.

The position of her arms about his neck prevented him from pushing the shoulder straps aside, while his lips on her skin caused quivers of excitement to shoot through her blood. The touch of his hands gently massaging the muscles of her back sent a searing desire leaping through her veins until suddenly she became aware of the warnings being shouted in her brain. They brought her to her senses, causing her to push against him and struggle from his arms.

He sat up, frowning at her angrily. 'Hell's teeth, do you always switch from positive to negative with such lightning speed?'

'Please, Brent . . .'

'I trust you don't imagine you're about to be manhandled?'

Lana sprang to her feet, then tightened the towelling girdle about her waist. 'I'm not waiting to find out. You work a little too fast for my liking. Besides, your *impulses* must be watched. They might run away with you.'

The last remark was flung over her shoulder as she turned and sped aross the sand towards the firmer shoreline near the water's edge. A quick glance over her shoulder indicated he had not followed her, nevertheless she continued to run along the beach until she reached the track leading up to the guest-house.

Minutes later she was in her room where she flung herself on the bed to relive the moments of Brent's arms holding her close to him. And while she stared at the ceiling seeing only his face above her, instinct warned she would be unwise to bask too often in delights of that nature. They could only finish in a dead end. No doubt Brent would lead her along, using a subtle step-by-step method until she was ready and willing to give him all she had been keeping for that very special man she expected to find some day.

Thinking of him, she knew that Brent was a special type of man who already loomed largely in her thoughts, but this whole situation was only temporary, because Peggy would return and then it would be time to go home. She would leave with nothing more than emptiness to clasp to her breast, memories that would torture her for ever more.

CHAPTER FOUR

SHE lay on the bed until she knew she must shower, then dress and go downstairs to face Brent, possibly to watch the scorn leap into his eyes while he thought of her as an idiotic fool who made a habit of running away, either down the stairs or along the beach. Where would she run next time? Or would there ever be a next time? Somehow she doubted it.

Confidence was what she needed, and after taking special care with her make-up she slipped into the satiny gold dress with the mandarin collar. It threw yellow lights into her hair and its sophisticated lines gave her an added beauty of which she was quite unaware.

When she went downstairs she found Eric and Hilary at the desk, both wearing frowns as they studied the register in which reservations were listed. Eric, who had been leaning over it, straightened his back as she approached, his eyes lighting with undisguised admiration. 'Well, just look at you, you're like a golden goddess,' he remarked with quiet sincerity.

Hilary sent him a sharp glance before she studied Lana's appearance 'Yes, very nice,' she admitted in a frigid tone.

'Is something wrong?' Lana asked, fearing that perhaps she had double-booked one of the rooms.

'We're short of a single room,' Hilary explained with a touch of irritation. 'Brent is adamant that you are not to be moved, but now that you're working at the desk I think you could occupy Peggy's room while she's away.'

'Of course. Naturally I should vacate a room that's

needed.'

Eric smiled his relief. 'I told you Lana wouldn't mind.'

'Yes, you did,' Hilary retorted snappishly. 'You appear to know her quite well. So that's settled, and it will solve this problem of a room for Camille.'

Lana was startled. 'Camille? You mean Mrs Boyd?'

'Yes. She often spends short periods here because it's more convenient than owning her own beach-house. Tomorrow morning you can move into the downstairs room next to the one Eric and I occupy. It's along the back passage in the staff quarters.'

'If you'll show it to me I'll move immediately,' Lana said with cool dignity, at the same time savouring the knowledge that Brent had not wished her to be moved.

'Right. Just follow me.' Hilary walked briskly towards a long passage at the rear of the building. Doors opened on either side, and she paused before the small room normally occupied by Peggy. 'I'm sure you will find this room quite comfortable, although it isn't blessed with an en-suite. The bathroom is further along the passage.'

'I'll be quite happy in it,' Lana assured her cheerfully.

As they returned to the passage Lana looked along its length and said, 'The staff quarters appear to be quite extensive.'

'They don't all live here. Some of them live in town and use their own transport,' Hilary explained, then added, 'That door at the end of the passage opens into Brent's apartment.'

The words died on her lips as the end door opened and Brent came through it. He was accompanied by Camille Boyd whose black and white outfit couldn't fail to catch the eye.

Hilary smiled as they approached. 'I'm putting Lana into Peggy's room, and then Camille can have the one Lana has been occupying. It'll be ready by ten o'clock in the morning.' She turned to Brent almost apologetically. 'I know you said Lana was not to be moved, but we had a room problem, and if Camille wishes to have a couple of weeks at the beach it would be a pity if we were unable to find accommodation for her.'

Camille said urgently, 'Of course, you must find a room for me, and as Lana is now staff she should be in the staff quarters, although I must admit she doesn't look like staff, at least not in *that* dress. It's much too opulent for the desk girl,' she added on a high note that betrayed jealousy.

Brent sent a surprised look towards Camille. 'You're forgetting that Lana came here as a guest,' he pointed out coldly, then turned to regard Lana with undisguised admiration.

She felt a glow rise into her cheeks. 'I'll make the change at once,' she promised hastily, then made her way to the room she had been occupying. Her belongings were crammed into her suitcase, the lid jammed down and the case carried to Peggy's room.

The changeover had taken only a short time, yet when she entered the dining-room she saw that Brent and Camille were already seated at the corner table while Eric sat alone at the one next to them. For a moment she played with the idea of joining him, until memory of Brent's remarks caused her to hesitate, and as she did so she was approached by Betty who gave her an apologetic smile.

'I'd better put you at this wall table,' the waitress said. 'As you can see, *she's* here again.'

'Don't you like her?' whispered Lana.

'Her superior attitude annoys me,' Betty retorted. 'Is it true she's booked in for another of her attempts to catch the boss?'

'Well, she's booked in,' Lana admitted with a rueful smile.

Betty left her to study the menu, but within a few

minutes she returned to whisper urgently. 'The boss wants you to join them at his table. Golly, I must say it's unusual.'

Lana glanced across the room then said, 'Please thank him for the invitation, but tell him I'm quite happy to remain here.'

Betty stared at her incredulously. 'You've got to be joking!'

'I'm serious, Betty. Just point out that I'm nicely settled at this table and have no intention of moving from it.'

Betty giggled. 'OK, I'll tell him.' She left to deliver the message, controlling her mirth with an effort.

Lana continued to examine the menu until a shadow fell across it. She looked up, startled to find Brent beside the table, his manner commanding as he leaned forward to speak in a low voice.

'Are you coming to my table, or do I have to carry you?'

She gave a short laugh. 'You wouldn't cause such a scene.'

'Wouldn't I? The guests would love it. It would give them something to talk about, especially if you'd be good enough to put on a show of screaming and kicking.'

'Aren't you forgetting that Camille won't want me at the table?'

'Camille's wishes don't happen to be the issue.'

'You mean you really want me at your table?'

'Of course.'

Lana capitulated, mainly because guests at nearby tables appeared to be watching them with interest, and as she crossed the room with him she became aware of the eyes that followed her. However, only Claramae Crosby nodded and smiled, then put out a hand to detain her.

'My dear, you look quite ravishing,' the American woman whispered earnestly. 'Just look at her, Elmer. Isn't she lovely?'

Elmer grinned. 'Sure is,' he mumbled with his mouth

full.

When they reached the table Camille's brittle smile consisted of little more than a flash of teeth. 'So sad to see you sitting alone,' she cooed in an audible voice. 'You looked almost *pathetic.*'

Her words carried to Eric at the next table which was close enough to enable matters to be discussed at mealtimes. He stood up and spoke to Camille. 'Do I also look pathetic sitting alone while Hilary is at the desk? Perhaps Lana would take pity on me.' He pulled out a chair as an invitation for her to sit with him.

She sent him a dazzling smile. 'Thank you, Eric, I'd love to keep you company,' she declared, sending a glance of defiance towards Brent, and although he made no comment she noticed the tightening of his mouth and knew he was annoyed.

During the meal Lana steered the conversation towards England, then encouraged Eric to talk about his life there. She knew that Brent watched them, and despite Camille's efforts to claim his attention he listened to every word that was being said.

Eventually Eric paused in his reminiscences. 'I'm afraid I've been boring you,' he apologised.

'Not at all,' Lana assured him hastily. 'I'm more interested than you can possibly imagine.'

'Really?' Eric was surprised.

Brent spoke from his nearby table, his tone ironical. 'Of course she is, old chap. Anyone with half an eye could see she was quite fascinated.'

She turned to look at him, wondering if her face had betrayed her inner feelings. She also realised she would learn no more of Eric's past for the moment, therefore she said, 'I'll go to the desk and relieve Hilary.'

But before she could move she became aware of Hilary watching them from the doorway, and as the older woman approached, her tight mouth made it obvious she was not amused by the sight of Lana sitting with her husband.

When Eric became aware of her presence he smiled blandly. 'Ah, there you are, my dear.'

'Yes, here I am,' Hilary snapped crossly. 'Isn't it time you allowed me to eat? I'm starving.'

Lana stood up. 'I'll take over for you. Eric hasn't finished his dessert.'

Camille laughed. 'That's because he's been talking too much,' she told Hilary sweetly. 'He's been telling Lana about his life in London, and believe me, she's been listening with bated breath. Isn't that so, Brent?'

Lana sent Camille a wide-eyed look of reproach, then flicked an anxious glance towards Brent. Had her interest in Eric been so obvious? But Brent's face had become inscrutable, and she guessed that, mentally, he was accusing her of paying too much attention to Hilary's husband. She turned and went towards the door, and as she left the room she could almost feel his accusations piercing her back.

The following days were uneventful. Guests came and went, and Lana noticed that Camille spent time in wandering about the place as though continually seeking Brent's company. But in this project she seemed to be unsuccessful because she was unable to deter him from giving his attention to matters concerning the farm or the guest-house.

The February warmth sent people to the beach, which meant there were always casuals in for lunch, and late one morning Lana looked up to discover two faces grinning at her from across the desk. Raewyn and Bronwyn, clad in their brightest sundresses, had arrived.

'We caught the bus,' Raewyn said. *'Where is he?'*

'Shut up,' Lana hissed furiously, thankful that Eric was busily engaged elsewhere.

'Doesn't he know who you are?' Bronwyn whispered.

'No, of course not, and if either of you dare to drop the slightest hint——'

'You'll cut our throats?' Raewyn grinned.

'They've got some mighty sharp knives in the kitchen, so be warned,' gritted Lana, glaring from one twin to the other.

Bronwyn giggled. 'Phooey to that for a load of rubbish. We know you're only bluffing. So what would you really do if we gave the show away?'

Lana considered them seriously. 'I'd refuse to live with you again,' she told them calmly. 'I'd find a flat of my own and I'd leave home.'

'You *wouldn't*,' they said, almost together.

'You just try me and see for yourselves. If you want me to leave home you know what to do.'

'Mum and Dad would be most upset,' Raewyn almost gasped.

'No doubt, and it would be the fault of the pair of you, so just watch your tongues.' Lana's voice held a warning ring.

'I believe she means it,' Bronwyn said. 'OK, Lana, we'll promise not to say a word to anyone. We do promise, don't we, Rae?'

Raewyn nodded. 'We won't breathe a word to a single soul,' she agreed. 'You know you can rely on us.'

'Can I? Unfortunately I'm not at all sure about that.' Lana retorted. Nor was she sure that she would really leave home, but in the meantime the threat would be effective—or so she hoped.

A long pause followed her last words while they looked at her in silence until Bronwyn said, 'Is there a food-shop near here? I'm hungry, absolutely *starving*.'

'So am I,' echoed Raewyn.

Lana shook her head. 'There's no shop nearer than the main road, but lunch will be on soon. Would you like to have a meal here? I'll take you to lunch.'

Their faces lit with satisfaction. 'Yes, please, that's really what we expected,' Raewyn admitted.

Hilary came at noon to take charge of the desk during Lana's lunch hour, and when the twins were introduced to her she made no attempt to disguise her surprise. 'Your sisters—with those brown eyes and such dark hair?' she exclaimed, looking at the two round faces. 'You're not even remotely alike.'

Bronwyn began to speak. 'Oh, we're not really——' then fell silent while casting a guilty look towards Lana.

Raewyn said hastily. 'We're like our mother. She's short and dark-haired, while Lana——' She paused uncertainly.

'While I have my father's colouring,' Lana finished for her with perfect truth. Then, in an attempt to hustle them away from the desk, 'I'd better give them food before they drop from starvation.'

Hilary smiled kindly. 'They can be guests of the house today. Give this to Betty.' She signed a chit and handed it to Lana.

'Oh, thank you.'

'Not at all. I'm sure Brent would want them to have lunch with you.' Hilary paused before sending Lana a hard look. 'I suppose you know Eric is away, that he's gone to Levin to see our accountant.'

The assumption behind her tone startled Lana. Had Hilary reached the stage of imagining that Eric confided his movements to her? she shook her head as she said, 'No, I had no idea.'

'He asked me to tell you there are letters waiting to be typed. They're on his desk.'

Lana smiled at her. 'Really? In that case, if he'd told me he was going to Levin, wouldn't he have also told me about the letters? I'll do them this afternoon.'

As they went towards the dining-room Bronwyn whispered, 'Is she your—your father's wife?'

'Yes.' The answer came abruptly.

'Then she's really your stepmother.'

'Yes, but she doesn't know it, so will you please drop the subject. Really, you're most irritating!'

Betty led them to a table in the centre of the room, and as they sat down Raewyn looked about her. 'The place is much larger than the usual guest-house,' she declared as though endowed with much knowledge concerning such matters.

Not to be outdone, Bronwyn agreed with her. 'You're right, Rae, it's more like a hotel.' She examined the other guests then leaned forward to speak to Lana in a low voice. 'Is he here—your father?'

'No. Didn't you hear Mrs Halversen say he's away in Levin?'

'Oh. So he's *Eric*?'

'Yes. Now please *shut up*,' Lana snapped. She glanced at the empty table usually occupied by the Halversens and in doing so she caught Brent's eye.

He was sitting with Camille, who had her back towards them, and Lana had a sudden suspicion he was curious about the two girls. This proved to be a fact when he appeared to excuse himself with a brief word, then stood up and came towards their table. Speaking to Lana he said, 'Am I right in assuming that these two young ladies are your sisters?'

The twins gaped at him, both turning scarlet as his dark eyes moved from one to the other, and then Raewyn, who was the first to regain her composure, asked breathlessly, 'Did Lana really tell you about us?'

'Of course she did. She said you were both growing up fast.'

Bronwyn was indignant. 'Growing up *fast*? Doesn't she know that we *are* grown up?'

Raewyn snapped at her twin, 'Drop it, Bron. We'll attend to it later.' She turned to dimple at Brent. 'Is it true you have horses here? I mean for guests to ride?'

'Yes.' He regarded her seriously. 'Do you ride?'

She shook her head sadly. 'There's no hope of learning to ride in the city, especially in a suburb where there's nothing but hilly tarmac roads and traffic.' Her eyes became soulful as she gave a deep sigh. 'It must be wonderful to ride along the beach.'

Bronwyn was quick to follow Raewyn's trend of thought. *'Really wonderful,'* she breathed with deep longing.

Brent laughed. 'OK, so what you'd really like is a ride along the beach, or am I mistaken about that?'

'Oh *please, please,'* they said together, joyful anticipation written on their faces.

Lana became impatient. 'This is ridiculous. They can't handle horses—they've never ridden in their lives.'

'Don't worry, I'll stay with them,' Brent assured her. 'I'll ride my own horse and put their mounts on leading reins just as I do for other non-riders.'

'It's very kind of you——' Lana began.

He waved her gratitude aside. 'An hour's ride along the beach should be sufficient to let them know they've been on a horse for the first time. Send them over to the stable at two o'clock.' Then favouring each of the twins with a brief nod he returned to his table.

They were speechless for several moments until Raewyn breathed, 'Cor, isn't he a hero out of a book! You know, I reckon he gave me a *special* look——'

Lana chuckled. 'Don't let yourself get a crush on him. He's too old for you, at least twice your age or more.'

'But he's not too old for you,' Bronwyn flashed at her. Her young face became serious. 'Do you like him, Lana?'

She lifted her shoulders in a casual gesture. 'I suppose he's—quite nice.' And that was an understatement, she admitted to herself. He was more than quite nice. He was kind and thoughtful, and definitely charming.

Nor was there any need for him to spend time in giving the twins a ride along the beach. They were not paying guests, so why should he bother unless—unless he planned to question them about herself? But no, that thought was ridiculous, because he had no real interest in her, especially with the attractive Camille Boyd nicely settled at his table.

Nevertheless when the time came to direct the twins to the stable she issued a warning, and eyeing them severely she said, 'Now don't forget, not a single word of discussion about me.'

They nodded vigorously, pulling on hats and slipping into jackets that matched their sundresses, and as they almost ran towards the back of the building Lana wondered if they had heard a word she had said.

She then set to work on the letters, but found concentration difficult because her mind was on the trio riding along the beach—or to be more exact upon one of the trio, because Brent loomed large in her thoughts. His face continually pushed its way between her and the paper in the typewriter, seeming to stare at her from the blank page.

And when it wasn't the vision of his face causing her to pause and gaze unseeingly at the wall, it was the memory of his arms holding her close to his body, first in the honeymoon suite, and secondly beside the sandhills edging the beach. Nor did the vivid recollection fail to provoke a sense of longing in her, a yearning that made her feel hot, and that was easily recognised as a desire for more.

Her state of mind caused her to make typing errors, and as she snatched the sheet of paper from the machine and inserted another an urgent tapping on the reception desk came to her ears. The diversion came as a relief until she went out to find herself faced by Camille, who made no effort to conceal her antagonism.

The green eyes became slightly narrowed as they surveyed Lana. 'You'd better know I'm not amused,' Camille snapped through tight lips. 'In fact I'm damned annoyed.'

Lana was taken aback but regarded her calmly. 'If something has upset you it'll be a case for Mrs Halversen.'

'It has nothing to do with Hilary, it's you and your wretched sisters. You had a colossal nerve upsetting my afternoon in this manner. I know perfectly well it was all your doing.'

Bewildered, Lana said, 'I'm afraid I don't know what you're talking about.'

'Oh yes, you do. You must have known that Brent had a fairly free afternoon and that we'd have plans for it. So what action do you take? You present him with the necessity to take people riding, your dratted sisters, no less. How very convenient to have them here at the right moment,' sneered Camille.

Lana was dismayed by the accusation. 'You've got it all wrong, Mrs Boyd,' she protested. 'I made no such arrangements.'

The thin lips curled with disdain. 'Of course you did. You booked them in for this afternoon, then beckoned to Brent from across the dining-room.'

'Did he tell you that?' Lana's tone held incredulity.

'He didn't have to. I can guess that much for myself,' Camille snapped. 'Brent is a very kind person, and you knew it would be the automatic course for him to take.'

Lana realised that explanations would be useless, nor, as a member of the staff, could she argue with a guest. However, she was unable to resist the temptation to fire a parting shot, and forcing a smile she said seriously, 'Mrs Boyd, if Brent had had plans with you for this afternoon he would not have changed them. There was no need for him to take my sisters riding. He could have arranged for them to be accompanied by the stableman who cares for the horses and who often takes people who are not used to riding.'

Camille's face betrayed her anger as she disgested this fact and realised its truth.

'I'm afraid this is a matter you'll have to take up with Brent,' Lana said, watching her expression. 'Now if you'll excuse me I have work to do.'

But when she returned to the typewriter concentration became even more difficult as her own words seemed to fling themselves in her face. Why had Brent taken the girls personally? As she herself had pointed out, he could have sent somebody else, not only the stableman but also the gardener, who often gave a hand with the horses and at times took guests for rides along the beach or over the farm. Therefore, had it been his intention to put a few quiet questions to the twins about her?

It was well after three o'clock before the twins returned, and despite a slight stiffness from the unaccustomed exercise they were delighted with their first experience of horse-riding.

'It was wonderful,' Raewyn exclaimed, her brown eyes shining, her face glowing. 'Gosh, he's *nice!*'

'You mean the horse?' Lana asked innocently.

'No, stupid, I mean Brent, of course. Can't you see that he's marvellous? He sure is Mr Gorgeous.'

'I really hadn't noticed,' Lana lied.

'Then wake up and look at him, dummy,' Raewyn snapped impatiently.

Bronwyn spoke in a voice brimming with confidence. 'We think he's interested in you. Isn't that so, Rae?'

'That's utter rubbish.' Lana's tone held amusement.

'I tell you he *is* interested,' Bronwyn persisted as she sent a veiled glance towards Raewyn. 'Don't we reckon so, Rae?'

'What gives you that daft idea?' Lana found difficulty in concealing her interest in this question.

'Because—well—just because.' Bronwyn looked down at her hands and lapsed into silence.

Lana detected guilt. 'I trust you're not hinting that I became part of the conversation,' she said, glaring suspiciously from one to the other. 'Didn't you girls promise that I would not be discussed?'

Raewyn put up a defence. 'But we had to answer his question, Lana. You wouldn't want us to be rude and just ignore it.'

Lana tried to control her growing apprehension. 'Question? What are you talking about? What was this question?'

Bronwyn said, 'Oh, it wasn't anything very much. He only wanted to know if your boyfriend was anxious to learn when you'd be coming home.'

'My—my boyfriend?'

'Yes. Well, we couldn't be rude and tell him to mind his own business, especially when he was giving us a ride along the beach,' Bronwyn explained. She paused, then added, 'Nor could we admit that you didn't even have a boyfriend. I mean, at your age it's quite embarrassing.'

'Is it, indeed?' snapped Lana, feeling irritated.

'Of course it is,' Raewyn agreed. 'So we explained to him that all your boyfriends kept phoning to ask when you'd be coming home.'

'*All* my boyfriends?' Lana echoed faintly. 'But that's a lie.'

'It's a white lie,' Bronwyn excused herself, as though this exonerated the untruth. 'We didn't want him to think you were neglected, so we explained that—that——'

Raewyn became impatient. 'So we explained that the men buzzed round you like flies round a honeypot. Really, Lana, there's no need to look like that.'

Bronwyn cut in, 'We did it for you, Lana. It was to hide the—the *shame* of—of not having a *real* boyfriend, and of looming towards being an old maid.'

'Spinster is the word,' Raewyn emphasised knowledge-ably.

Lana began to see the funny side of the situation, but the laughter that shook her was silenced abruptly by Raewyn's next words.

'We also told him that all the men who took you out were old, like himself, or even older.'

'And that's when we knew he was really interested in you,' Bronwyn added eagerly. 'It was the look on his face. We both noticed it, didn't we, Rae?'

Raewyn nodded. 'That was when he said it was time to turn the horses for home. After that he went sort of quiet.'

Lana found difficulty in controlling her wrath, but she managed to say calmly, 'And that's all? You had no further information to give him concerning my personal love-life?'

They shook their heads and then Raewyn said, 'In fact he was so quiet all the way home we knew he must be thinking about you. Didn't we, Bron?'

'There'll be no doubt about that,' Lana remarked with a sinking feeling of resignation. Obviously the twins had given him plenty to think about, mainly through their assertion of her preference for older men. *Older men like Eric,* he would tell himself.

But they had been working on her behalf, she admitted mentally, so she must not hurt them by revealing the inner dismay that was beginning to form like an icy ball somewhere near the pit of her stomach, and at last she said, 'I think it's time you went home. Mother is sure to worry if you're late.'

Bronwyn said, 'We've decided to come again, haven't we, Rae?'

Raewyn nodded. 'Yes, we'll be back quite soon.'

Fond of them as she was, Lana's spirits sank at the prospect, and even as they looked at her expectantly she decided to nip their plan before it could blossom. So she said with quiet determination, 'Very well, but when you come again be sure to bring plenty of money, because you'll each have to pay for your own meal in the dining-rom, and for the hire of the horses. This is not a charitable institution for teenagers.'

Their indignation was voiced by Raewyn. 'Are you saying you won't pay for us?'

'That's right. Today you just happened to be lucky.'

'After all Rae and I have done for you,' Bronwyn exclaimed in a shocked tone. 'Talk about *gratitude*!'

'I can live without your assistance, thank you,' Lana told them. 'Now see that you drive home carefully.'

'You're jealous,' Bronwyn exploded. 'You don't want us to go riding with him.'

'Don't be stupid,' Lana retorted angrily. 'And for heaven's sake keep your voice down. You talk too much and it's all rubbish.'

'Huh! Rubbish, is it?'

Raewyn took her twin's arm. 'Come along, Bron, let's go home. Anyone can see we're not wanted here, even after we've done so much.'

'You can say that again,' said Lana with controlled fury.

She followed them through the front entrance and was greeted by the sight of Brent sitting at one of the nearby lawn tables. He was accompanied by Camille who, sheltered by the large umbrella, leaned her elbows on the table and smiled as she chatted animatedly.

Their apparent intimacy caused an unexpected depression to settle upon Lana and she turned her face away as she accompanied the twins to the bus stop. They also had done their share to make her feel depressed, and while she regretted the need to snap at them, she was anxious to see them heading for home.

But before the two girls could get into the bus they saw

Brent. A swift glance passed between them and then Raewyn, who usually took the lead, waved to him. 'Goodbye, Brent,' she called. 'Lana is worried in case we haven't thanked you for our lovely rides. Please come and tell her that we really did thank you.'

He muttered a word to Camille, then stood up and came towards them.

'She's insisting that we do so again,' Bronwyn lied as he drew near to them.

He frowned at Lana. 'Of course they thanked me. In any case, I'm not looking for gratitude.'

'I don't think she wants us to come here again,' Bronwyn told him in a voice full of pathos.

'Oh? Why would that be?' He was still frowning at Lana.

Raewyn said quickly, 'She says we talk too much. She says we shouldn't have told you about her having so many—*friends*.'

He grinned. 'Oh yes, all those old men!'

Lana began to feel hysterical. Laughter shook her, and as the bus drove away her mirth became almost uncontrollable.

Brent looked at her with concern. 'What the devil is so funny?'

'I don't think—you'd understand. You'd better so back to—to Camille.'

'Right, I'll do that.' He left her and returned to the table where he sat with his back turned towards her.

The action gave her the feeling of having been dismissed, but after all, what else could she expect from this lord of the lodge?

CHAPTER FIVE

THE following days left Lana with little time to brood over the wrong impressions the twins might have given Brent. She found herself busily engaged with more office work than she had expected, and although this fact placed her near him it did nothing to improve or dispel the rather tense relationship that seemed to have developed between them.

She became increasingly aware that he had little to say while sitting with his head bent, his eyes moving from sheets of paper to his calculator, and she guessed he was preparing figures to be taken to his accountant. Nevertheless she felt he could have sent the odd friendly word in her direction, but although she waited hopefully for it to be uttered, no sound of it came to her ears.

Frustrated, she continued with the task of typing answers to queries concerning the cost of fishing-trips to Kapiti, and the suitability of bush walks for older people. At times she had to confer with Eric, and it was during one of these occasions that she realised she was not being completely ignored by Brent. From the corner of her eye she watched him observing her attitude towards Eric, and the knowledge filled her with irritation.

However, she brushed it aside as she sat down to answer a query concerning the horses. She was then reminded of the twins and their joy at being on horseback, and as she thought of them a smile touched her lips.

Brent noticed it. 'Something is amusing you?'

'Yes.' Her smile broadened, and although the question had surprised her she did not enlighten him because to do so would only remind him of the twins' silly babblings

79

about her preference for older men.

'What's that particular query about?' he demanded abruptly.

'Oh, it's just about the horses.'

'Horses? Isn't that my department? Shouldn't I have been consulted rather than Eric?' His tone has become sharp. 'I've watched your *tête-à-têtes* over those letters, heads together like a pair of conspirators.'

Lana was startled by the strangely cold glint in his eyes, the cynical twist to his mouth. The antagonism behind his expression shook her as she tried to explain, 'You appeared to be so busy, I presumed you had no wish to be disturbed. You were so silent, so remote.'

There was a moment's silence while his eyes moved from her face to Eric's, and as they did so his expression changed to one of mild surprise as he said, 'Did you know there's a definite likeness between you? Similar colouring, same straight noses—'

Lana's heart skipped a beat while she forced a light laugh and brushed the suggestion aside. 'It's only because we both have such fair hair,' she assured him.

'Take no notice,' Eric advised her. 'It's just Brent's subtle form of insult. Who on earth would want to think they look like me?'

'He's fishing for a compliment,' Brent grinned at Lana, his good humour seemingly restored. 'He's really asking to be told he's a good-looking fellow, handsome, in fact.'

Lana ignored the banter between them as she sprang to Eric's defence. 'Why not be honest and admit that he is a handsome man?' she asked unguardedly.

Brent raised an eyebrow. 'You really think so? Is that why I suspect there's an affinity between you?'

'That's utter nonsense,' she snapped angrily.

'Try to ignore his remarks,' Eric suggested smoothly. 'I've a strong suspicion he's jealous. Perhaps I should watch out for repercussions,' he added with a grin.

'Particularly from Hilary,' Brent cut in, his voice again cold.

Lana became impatient. 'I don't like the trend of this conversation.' She swung round to face Brent, her blue eyes sparkling with anger. 'As for your insinuations that I have designs upon Eric, you'd better believe that you're entirely mistaken.'

Eric shook his head in mock sorrow. 'That's very sad. I'd like to imagine that a lovely young woman like Lana had designs upon me.'

She flashed a smile at him as she stretched out a hand to pat his arm. 'Never mind, I'll look upon you as a kindly father figure.' The words died on her lips as she wondered how many more foolish statements she would make before leaving Leisure Lodge. Then drawing a deep breath she turned to Brent and said, 'Would you like to check this query about the horses? It's just——'

'I'll leave it to you—and Eric,' he snapped tersely.

Brent's attitude and his veiled suggestion of a growing alliance between Eric and her was disturbing, and while she was vitally conscious of his presence she did not speak to him again before returning to the reception desk. Nor, it seemed, did he wish to speak to her, and she felt his silence wrapping itself about her like a cloak of cold disapproval. Not that she really cared, of course.

However, when Hilary came to take a turn at the desk she looked at Lana critically, then asked, 'Is there a problem?'

Lana was surprised by the question. 'No. What makes you think there could be a problem?'

'You have a dejected air about you. Perhaps you're becoming bored with this job. I'm afraid it'll be another two weeks or more before Peggy returns.'

'I'm not even remotely bored,' Lana hastened to assure her. 'I said goodbye to the couple who left from number six, and I've had to decide where to put two new couples who arrived without having previously made reservations.'

A look of annoyance crossed Hilary's face. '*You* decided? What made you think you had the right to decide where they should be put? You should have called me.'

Lana was taken aback by her attitude. 'I made sure the two rooms emptied this morning had been prepared.'

'Really! You *are* learning the running of the place. Do you expect to take over at some future date?' Hilary demanded crossly.

'No, of course not.' Lana fell silent, lost for words.

'In future please make an effort to find me.' The words were snapped furiously as Hilary glared at her.

The older woman's barely controlled anger bewildered Lana, but she retained her dignity as she said, 'I'm sorry if I've done the wrong thing, but at least I did ask Eric. It was after I'd finished his letters——'

'Ah, so he's had you in there with him again.' Hilary's eyes narrowed slightly. 'It's becoming a frequent task, I notice.'

'Yes. I'm glad I can do more than attend to the reception desk.'

'No doubt you enjoy being in there with him.' Hilary's eyes glittered as her words came icily.

Lana decided to ignore the innuendo that hinted she was more than partial to Eric's company. 'Brent was there also, busy with farm accounts,' she said with controlled calm.

'You should be looking at Brent, rather than at Eric,' Hilary told her bluntly.

Lana's tone became cool. 'Please understand that I am not looking at Eric. He's—he's far too old for me.'

'Some girls like older men,'

'I'm not one of them,' Lana told her sharply.

'But surely you must realise—he's looking at you.'

'Isn't that because I remind him of—of someone?'

'Yes, Ingrid, his first wife. Apparently your likeness to her fascinates him. He can't keep his eyes off you, and I strongly suspect he likes you to be near him.' Hilary's anger rang clearly.

Lana was silent, unable to find words that would deny these facts which had become obvious even to herself. Eventually she said, 'I'm sure it's only that he needs help with the typing.'

'Humbug!' Hilary snorted. 'Eric is perfectly capable of typing letters, although not as quickly as you do them, of course.'

Lana was surprised. 'I thought Peggy did them.'

'Only occasionally. He has never used her typing ability to the extent that he's using yours. So how do you think all this affects me?' Hilary pursued. 'I'm losing him to you, and all because of your similarity to Ingrid. Really, it's quite ridiculous.'

Lana took a deep breath as she sought for reassuring words. 'Honestly, there's no need for you to worry, particularly as I'll be leaving as soon as Peggy returns.'

'By that time Eric will have reached the stage of not wanting you to go,' Hilary told her bitterly. 'He was so very much in love with Ingrid. It took him years to get over her death, and now it's almost as if her ghost has arisen to confront him. It's as if all the loving care I've given him has been wiped away by a face from the past.' Sudden tears filled her eyes.

Lana bit her lip as she looked down at her hands, and although she searched for words she could find nothing to say. She was also troubled by a fact that hit her with sudden force. She had made a mistake in coming here. Her dream of learning about her roots had caused her to ignore the possibility of creating unhappiness for other people.

But at that time she hadn't expected to stay here. Her intention had been only to look at her natural father, perhaps talk to him briefly, and then return home to Wellington. It had been Peggy's annual vacation, her sister's wedding and her determination to be with her family at Bluff that had altered the whole situation.

During their conversation the door into the office had remained closed, but now it opened abruptly and Brent emerged. He passed the desk with barely a glance at either Lana or Hilary, and as he strode along the passage towards the staff quarters the older woman said with conviction, 'He's annoyed about something. I feel sure he's had an argument with Eric.'

Lana said nothing, but was assailed by a strong suspicion that she herself had been the cause of angry words passing between the two men. The fact that Brent had ignored her made her feel as if he had dealt her a snub, the sting of it causing her to say, 'Perhaps it would be better if I leave tomorrow.'

Hilary was startled. 'Tomorrow? Oh no, please don't go so suddenly or Eric will blame me. He'll know I'm jealous and—and besides—we do need you.'

But Lana's thoughts were not with Eric. They were with Brent and his attitude towards her, which was more upsetting than she cared to admit. The problem was that she liked him, and she also knew she wanted him to like her, but this was unlikely to happen while he believed her to be emotionally involved with Eric.

At last she said, 'I'll have to think about it. I'll go for a walk and let it swim round in my mind.'

'Can you ride a bicycle?' Hilary asked unexpectedly. 'There are a couple of them in the back shed, a lady's and a gent's. Staff sometimes use them to ride over to the farmhouse for extra milk or cream. A bike ride would be a change from walking along the beach,' she added with a smile.

Lana's face lit at the prospect. 'I haven't tried to ride a

bike for years,' she said. 'At least, not since I stayed with
Father's relatives in Christchurch where the land is so flat.'

Hilary sent her a curious look. 'Surely your father's relatives
are your relatives as well?'

'Oh, yes, I suppose they are,' she said, casually brushing the
question aside while knowing it was impossible to explain her
inner feelings on this matter, least of all to Hilary Halversen.
Then, aware of Hilary's hazel eyes still regarding her intently,
she said, 'I'll probably fall off the bike, no matter how hard I
try to stay on.'

'A little practice is all you need. There's a metal road
between the guest-house and the farm manager's home, but
make sure you don't get into the loose sand on either side of it.'

'It'll give me something soft to fall into,' Lana replied, her
natural cheerfulness asserting itself over her former dejection.

She left Hilary to go to her room where she changed into a
pair of blue jeans and a red jersey for protection against the
cool southerly breeze that had sprung up. And although the
sun's rays had lost their intensity she pulled on a wide-
brimmed straw sunhat with red ribbons that tied beneath her
chin.

Surveying herself in the mirror, she decided she looked like a
pathetic child and that the floppy hat did not go well with the
jeans. But what did it matter? There was nobody to criticise
her appearance, nor was she likely to meet anybody on the
road which twisted through the sandhills lying between the
guest-house and the farm buildings. In any case very little of
the road could be seen from the windows.

Her supposition that she would not be seen by anyone
proved to be wrong almost immediately, because as soon as she
stepped into the staff quarters passageway she discovered
Camille knocking discreetly on the door of Brent's apartment.
Also, the back deliberately turned towards her indicated that
Camille did not intend to speak, but this action prompted
Lana to pause and say, 'Don't tell me, let me guess—you're

looking for Brent.'

Camille sent her a haughty stare, and at that moment the door opened to reveal Brent. He stood aside as Camille went into his living-room, and although Lana expected him to close the door he merely stood and looked at her. His eyes took in her wide-brimmed hat, the stretch of red jersey that emphasised her breasts. The slimness of her waist and hips beneath her jeans came in for his attention until at last he demanded curtly, 'Where are you going?'

'For a bike ride. Hilary suggested it, so I presume it's permissible.' Her cheeks felt warm beneath his scrutiny.

'Brent dear!' Camille's plaintive voice came from behind him.

Lana was unable to resist an amused laugh. 'You'd better run along. You're being called.' The smile on her face belied the sudden and unexpected ache that began to manifest itself somewhere deep within her breast.

It caused her to turn blindly towards the nearby door that led outside, and once in the open air she took several deep breaths to conquer the moisture that was perilously near her eyes. In an effort to brush it away she blinked rapidly, then walked along a path to examine the garden which, on this side of the wide-fronted guest-house, was sheltered from the harsh winds that swept in from the sea.

Good soil added to the sand enabled a profusion of flowers to bloom, and a riot of brilliant marigolds formed a border for the taller red, yellow and pink canna lilies. Patches of purple climbing geraniums added splashes of contrasting colour, and she was admiring a bed of fluffy asters when a voice spoke from behind her.

'You like the flowers, miss?'

She swung round to face Bert, the middle-aged man who attended to the garden between other tasks involving the horses and farm. 'Oh, yes, they're lovely. You've made a real show.'

'Would you like a few for your room?'

'Thank you, I'd love some when I come back, but at the moment I'm going for a bike ride along the farm road.'

'Then I'll pump the tyres for you.'

Lana's depression lifted as she followed him towards the shed. A bike ride in the late afternoon sun was exactly what she needed to remove Brent's face from her mind and the thought of his cosy, to say nothing of secluded, *tête-à-tête* with Camille.

A short time later she was pedalling along the narrow road that had been formed between the low sandhills. At first she had wobbled badly from side to side, but after a little assistance from Bert in getting started her confidence mounted and she rode steadily with the wind at her back.

However, it was not for long, because she hadn't gone far when her hat proved to be her undoing. The ribbon securing it safely to her head had no control over the wide brim which the breeze caused to flap in her face, and at times it shielded her vision. In an unguarded moment she went too near the edge of the road and the next instant the front wheel left the firm surface and plunged into the soft sand.

A neat dive sent her over the handlebars to be flung against a low marram-grass-covered mound, and there she lay, unhurt but shaken by the sudden impact. The wheels of the bicycle continued to spin helplessly, and extricating herself from it she sat up and pushed it away from her.

She then lay back to relax for a short time, and as she watched clouds drifting overhead she basked in the last of the sun's warmth. Another day had flown past, she thought sadly, closing her eyes. It was another day nearer Peggy's return from the South Island, and another day nearer her own return to Wellington.

And it was then that she realised she liked this place. She enjoyed the contact with the guests who came and went, and with the various members of the staff. It was so much more enjoyable than being cooped up in an office while

Wellington's wind howled round the city's tall buildings, with little or no opportunity to breathe in sun or walk on the beach.

At least these were the reasons she gave herself for her reluctance to leave Leisure Lodge. It had nothing to do with Brent, although the vision of his handsome face kept pushing itself into her thoughts, and while she made a fruitless effort to keep him out of her ponderings she told herself he had nothing, *absolutely nothing*, to do with her desire to remain. And even as she emphasised this decision to herself her ears were assailed by the sound of his voice.

'You've had a tumble. Are you all right? You're able to get up?'

She sat up abruptly. 'I took a flying leap. I hope the bike isn't damaged.'

He examined it. 'Not even a loose spoke in the wheel.'

She looked at the bike he was riding. When last seen, Bert had been pumping its tyres. 'Are you on your way to the farmhouse?'

'No. I came to see what had happened to you. I was at the window watching your hat appearing and then disappearing between the sand hills, but suddenly it disappeared at a place where I should have been able to see it. I felt something was wrong, so I grabbed this gent's bike from the shed and came to investigate.'

Lana felt pleased by his concern. 'That was kind of you. You actually left Camille to make sure I was all right.'

'Why should my concern surprise you?' Frowning, he sat down beside her, then turned to regard her intently. 'Aren't you forgetting that the welfare of everyone at this place is my concern?'

Conscious of the tingle caused by his nearness, she said, 'That's quite understandable, regarding your guests and permanent staff, but I don't come into either category. Besides, it's become more than obvious that you disapprove of me. Or did you imagine I hadn't noticed?'

He sent her a slanting glance. 'My approval is important to you?'

She stared straight ahead. 'Let's say that I feel your dis-approval to be unjust. And apart from that, your thoughts appear to be very much with Camille. She'll be furious with me for taking you away from her, especially as you were probably enjoying a cosy little chat in your apartment or suite or whatever.'

'It's merely a living-room, bedroom and bathroom, and not half as opulent as the honeymoon suite.' He turned to rest on one hip, then his hand reached out to trail gentle fingers down her cheek. 'You do remember the honeymoon suite? Yes, of course you do, it's making you blush.'

Lana was annoyed to know that colour had risen to her face, but she tried to excuse it by saying in an offhand manner, 'There are times when I blush profusely, almost for no reason at all, and then the twins declare I look like a ripe tomato wearing a blonde wig.'

'An incorrigible pair,' he remarked, edging slightly closer.

'With vivid imaginations to match. I hope you realise that their tales concerning me are not to be taken seriously. They're only fifteen and they like to romance.'

His hand moved to rest upon her arm. 'Does this mean there isn't a line-up of young men eagerly awaiting your return?'

She laughed, wishing she could control the sensation caused by his touch. 'If there is I don't know who they are.'

Brent's expression hardened as the grip on her arm became stronger. 'In that case their statement about your preference for *older* men is correct?'

'Not at all,' she retorted, snatching her arm away and infuriated by the turn of the conversation.

He continued to regard her with a narrowed gaze that was full of questions until he said, 'I can't help feeling puzzled about you.'

She remained calm. 'What could possibly puzzle you about

me?'

'To begin with, your choice of Leisure Lodge as a holiday place. Haven't you noticed that the guests are mainly middle-aged or elderly people whose requirements do not include the deafening music preferred by the younger set of today?'

'I'm not a loud-noise type of person. I prefer easy listening.'

'Nevertheless, I'd have thought a place with more activity woudl have drawn you towards it. And having realised that Leisure Lodge is not overrun with the younger set I'd have thought you'd have gone searching for it elsewhere.'

'Aren't you forgetting Peggy, and Hilary's need for assistance?'

'Indeed I am not, because that's another puzzling point. If I recall the situation correctly it was you who offered to help.'

Lana turned to him, wide-eyed. 'Are you suggesting I snatched at an opportunity to remain here?'

He said nothing, his eyes like spears that dug for the truth.

'Why would I need a reason to stay? I could have just remained as a guest.' It was a half-truth only, and she knew it, And then her anger mounted. 'You think I extended my stay in this place for an ulterior motive,' she accused him as the suspicion grew stronger.

'I didn't say that.' He was still watching her narrowly.

'You don't have to. It's written all over your face, and what's more I can follow the trend of your thoughts. You think I stayed because of Eric.'

'Well, didn't you?'

'Yes.' The word slipped out unguardedly. 'But not in the way you imagine,' she amended, furious with herself for making even the slightest affirmation of this fact.

'So there is something. Care to tell me about it?'

'Certainly not. It's my own private business and I intend to keep it that way.' Her voice trembled slightly and she feared he would drag further information from her if she remained, so she made an attempt to get to her feet.

But his firm grip on her arm anchored her against the sandhill. His touch sparked a flash of electricity through her veins while his eyes held a strange intensity as they scanned the clear complexion of her face. His mouth came perilously near hers, hovering above it until she was sure he was about to kiss her, but in this she was mistaken, and she became aware of a sudden and searing disappointment.

His voice came softly. 'Tell me, what has Eric got that I haven't got?'

'To begin with, he's got Hilary,' she prevaricated.

'You know what I mean,' he persisted.

'For another thing, there's a gentleness about him. I doubt that he'd grab my arm and grip it until it hurt.' Lana looked down at the tanned fingers that continued to encircle her wrist.

He released her arm abruptly, then frowned at the marks caused by the strength of his fingers. 'The bruise, if there is one, will serve to remind you that I happen to be around,' he told her brusquely.

Her glare held defiance. 'I understand. You'll be around spying and watching my movements where Eric is concerned,' she suggested coldly, her spirits drooping.

'If necessary,' he warned in a nonchalant voice. 'Perhaps I should remind you that your thinly veiled obsession with Eric could affect the smooth running of the lodge, and that's something I'll not tolerate. Your cosy little chats with him are becoming so very frequent they're developing into a series of getting-to-know-you sessions.'

His nearness to the truth caused her to smile inwardly, but her face remained serious as she said, 'For Pete's sake, Eric has merely been telling me about Norway. Is that something to send you into a mad frenzy that makes you jump up and down?' Her tone rang with scorn.

'Norway? You're particularly interested in that country?'

'Well, yes, I am.'

'Is it because you've learnt he happens to be of Norwegian

descent?' The question was heavily tinged with sarcasm.

'Not at all, although I was interested to learn my blonde colouring makes me look like a Norwegian girl.'

'He's an authority on Norwegian girls?' The words were accompanied by a low laugh.

Lana ignored his mockery. 'At least he's been there and has seen a few of them.' She sighed, then added, 'Norway must be quite beautiful with its mountains and fjords. I'd love to see the midnight sun and the northern lights.'

'I wasn't aware that Eric knew so much about the country.'

'He told me he went there years ago to search for places where his own forebears had lived before leaving for New Zealand.'

'He found them?'

'Yes. He was able to describe the areas to me and even the type of houses they lived in.' She glowed inwardly at the recollection of all she had learnt, and now she found difficulty in hiding her delight in the information her gentle probing had brought forth. It had given her knowledge about her own forebears, and had opened her ancestral door a little wider.

Brent's lips twisted into an ironic smile. 'In less than two weeks you appear to have learnt more about Eric then I've discovered in years. You've really drawn him out.'

'At least you should be able to see that there's been nothing in our conversations to cause trouble, no reason for anyone to get uptight or their hair in a knot.'

'I'll try to believe you.' The lines about his mouth were still grim, while his eyes continued to reflect doubt.

A thought startled her, giving her the opportunity to change the subject. 'Aren't you forgetting Camille? Has she been waiting in your room all this time?'

'Certainly not. Camille came to borrow a book on the history of this coastal area. I gave it to her and she took it to her room. Did you imagine something—more intimate?' A faint smile touched his lips as he asked the question.

'Why not? You've been very sure of a growing intimacy between Eric and me,' she retorted, her tone cool.

'Point taken,' he replied drily.

Lana looked at the sardonic expression settling about his mouth and caught a glitter from eyes that were again narrowed in thought. The suspicion that more argument concerning Eric was about to break forth assailed her, and, grasping at the first idea to enter her mind, she said, 'What's the name of the book you've lent to Camille?'

'It's entitled *The Kapiti Coast*. Before the white people came to this coastal strip the land was populated by Maori tribes who fought among themselves like wild dogs, at least until a chief named Te Rauparaha came from the north and subjugated the lot. From then on he ruled the area.'

'Te Rauparaha. I remember reading about him at school.'

'A ruthless individual, and although not born to the highest chiefly rank he clawed his way to the top by cunning strategy, audacity and ferocious bloodshed.'

'A charming fellow,' Lana said with a sudder, then looked at Brent with sudden insight. 'I believe Maori history is a subject that interests you. Please tell me more.'

'Well, Kapiti Island became his stronghold, and then, during the 1830s, the early churchmen in New Zealand were informed that he desired the presence of a missionary in this area. The request resulted in the arrival of the Reverend Octavius Hadfield who came from Bay of Islands to establish a mission station and a school, and who taught the Maori people all he knew. It was he who had the famous Maori church built at Otaki.'

'The American lady, Mrs Crosby, asked me about it. I said you'd tell her how to reach it.'

'I've promised to drive them to see it tomorrow. Would you like to come with us?'

Lana was so amazed by the invitation she could only stare at him in speechless wonder.

'Well?' Brent demanded impatiently.

'You're forgetting I have to be at the desk,' she pointed out.

'You've been at the desk every day since Peggy left for her holiday. We don't crack the whip all the time, and you're due for a few hours off. I'll arrange with Hilary to take over from you.'

She was unable to resist the question that slipped off her tongue.

'Are you sure you wouldn't prefer to take Camille?'

'Would I have asked you if that had been the case?'

'The invitation might have been given impulsively, and if so I'll quite understand, so please don't hesitate to say so.'

'If you don't want to come why not be frank about it?'

'Oh, but I do want to come.'

'Then why all this shilly-shally? Or is it that you'd rather stay near Eric?' The second question was snapped abruptly.

She was appalled by the suggestion. 'No—no, of course not.'

'Very well, we'll leave after lunch tomorrow.' Brent stood up and held out a hand to pull her to her feet.

His firm grip seemed to send fire shooting up her arm and she found herself unable to look at him lest he guessed her stirrings of inner excitement. Tomorrow she would be going out with him, but why should anticipation of such a simple event affect her in this way? Why should it loom before her as something to be looked forward to? After all, it was only a visit to a church in the company of other people, so why the ridiculous confusion in her mind?

As they rode back towards the guesthouse Brent said casually, 'I have a booklet which gives information about Rangiatea.'

'Rangiatea? That's the name of the church?'

'Yes. It means the Abode of the Absolute.'

The glance she sent him was full of understanding. 'I have a suspicion that this church really means something to you.'

He nodded. 'It's part of the coast's history, as well as being a church with its own unique atmosphere. You'll feel it the moment you walk in the door.'

She did not answer, mainly because she was finding it necessary to concentrate on riding the bicycle. The wind was now in their faces, and her hat flapped at the back of her shoulders. It would be quite ghastly to have another mishap before his eyes, and she was thankful when they reached the shed and replaced the bicycles.

As they crossed the yard she realised that members of the kitchen staff were observing them through a window, and Lena assured herself their interest stemmed from the fact that they were not accustomed to seeing their boss ride a bicycle. His transport was normally the smart Jaguar she had noticed in his private garage, or perhaps it was the large station wagon parked beside it.

When they reached the door of the staff quarters Brent said, 'I'd like you to come into my apartment while I find that booklet. If you study it this evening it will help you to understand all that you see tomorrow.'

He opened the door, then stood aside while she entered a room dominated by its atmosphere of male occupation. The living-room was brown, relieved by gold in the carpet and curtains. Easy chairs upholstered in leather were placed at strategic points for viewing television, or for reading books selected from an extensive collection of volumes.

He said, 'May I offer you a drink? I'm sure you could do with a pick-me-up after being tossed into the sand. Scotch, sherry, or gin sling?'

Lana smiled. 'I'm well over that tumble, but yes, a sherry would be nice, thank you.'

She placed her hat on a chair, and while he became busy at a drinks cabinet she examined the pictures on the walls. Most of them were original paintings, scenes of early New Zealand in oils or watercolours. Each seemed to convey its own message, suggesting that its owner held a love for earlier traditions, and, recalling Brent's self-confessed interested in the district's history, she suddenly felt that she knew him better.

One oil painting hanging above the mantelpiece was different from the rest because instead of being a landscape it was a portrait. She moved closer to gaze up at it and was struck by its likeness to Brent. The eyes that stared back at her could have been his, especially when they took on their penetrating expression, and she was forced to ask, 'Is this a portrait of your father?'

'No. He was my father's brother, my Uncle James from whom I inherited Leisure Lodge.' He handed a glass of sherry to Lana, then raised his own Scotch towards the portrait. 'To you, Uncle James,' he said by way of a toast. 'Thank you again. Be assured I'll take good care of the place. There'll be no spanner thrown into the works.

She turned to look at him, her eyes shadowed. 'That last sentence contained a ring of familiarity. Was it directed to your uncle, or was it a dirty big hint directed at me?'

His dark eyes regarded her for several moments, their expression unfathomable until he turned again to the portrait. Speaking to it he said, 'What do you think, Uncle? Is it possible for her to throw old Eric off balance?'

Lana sipped her sherry, at the same time becoming acutely aware of the aura of male magnetism that seemed to draw her to this man. 'Well, what does he say?' she asked at last.

'I'm not sure,' he admitted. 'I just get a strong feeling that he's definitely warning me.'

Her chin rose. 'How very interesting. Against what? Or against whom, may I ask?'

He turned to regard her intently. 'Perhaps you could help me to find the answer to those questions.'

CHAPTER SIX

BRENT carried a finely cut crystal sherry decanter across the room. He refilled Lana's empty glass and said, 'Have another drink. You can't fly on one wing, besides, it'll help you to think.'

She looked at the almost brimming glass of golden liquid. 'Think? What do you mean?'

'I mean it'll help you to assist me.'

'I'm afraid I don't understand. How can I assist you?'

'I need the answers to those questions. My uncle is warning me—against what? The message comes through quite clearly.'

A gurgle of laughter escaped her. 'I see. And you're hoping the sherry will make me talkative.' She took a few sips, then looked at him across the top of the glass. 'The answer is obvious. Your uncle is warning you against your own imagination. It's running away with you. As for anything else, only time will tell, and time is moving along rapidly. The days are speeding towards Peggy's return and then I'll be gone. Your worries concerning Eric and me will be over.'

Although her last words were spoken flippantly, Lana was conscious of an inner despondency. What she had said was all too true. She would disappear from Eric's sight, but would the man standing before her disappear from her mind? Despite her efforts he was now dominating her thoughts in a most disturbing manner, invading them to a greater extent than any other man she had ever known.

At the same time she tried to tell herself it was mere infatuation because, after all, he was the most handsome man she had ever known. He was a man whose virility reached out to touch those around him, and while she recognised this fact she continued to assure herself she was merely suffering from a severe bout of infatuation.

Almost as though she had no control over her movements, she turned to look at him and was startled to find he had moved closer to her. Her eyes widened, and perhaps it was their unguarded expression that caused him to take the glass from her hand and place it beside his own on a small table. His hands then went to her shoulders, the firmness of their grip almost making her catch her breath, and as he drew her against him his arms encircled her body.

She knew she should protest, but she also knew she had no wish to do so, and as his mouth came down to meet her uplifted lips her heart seemed to leap into a bouncing thump that sent the blood hurtling through her veins. Push him away, you fool, she told herself in a dreamy haze. But instead of obeying common sense her arms crept about his neck while she gave herself up to the joy of being held closely, and to the blissful feel of his strong fingers gently massaging the muscles along her spine.

As the kiss ended he continued to hold her against him. 'Just relax,' he advised in a low voice. 'You're always so tense, almost as though you're ill at ease.'

He was perceptive, she realised, closing her eyes as she leaned her head against his broad shoulder. But how could she explain that she held a constant fear of her true relationship to Eric being discovered?

In searching for an excuse she said, 'Sometimes you make me feel nervous.' It was true. This man had an effect that made her wonder about herself, because almost from the moment of meeting him she had become conscious of her quickening pulses whenever he was near.

He said, 'There's no need to be nervous at the moment. This isn't the honeymoon suite.'

'No, but it's your own private lair.'

'Let me assure you it's only a place where two people can talk in private and get to know each other.'

Her heart gave a lurch but she managed to ask calmly, 'Are you suggesting that we should get to know each other better?'

'At the moment that happens to be my intention.' Brent looked at her intently, then added, 'It hasn't been so easy to get to know you at the desk or in the office, especially with Eric gawping at you and you looking at him.'

She laughed shakily. 'Haven't I told you it's not what you think?'

'It's not what I *think*, it's what I *see* that concerns me. And perhaps you should be warned that it has also become obvious to Hilary.'

'Really?' There was no need to admit she was already aware of this fact, she decided. It could only lead to more questions.

'Have you ever heard of a wife putting her husband through the meat-mincer?' he pursued. 'We've a good one in the kitchen. I'm telling you, she'll be glad to see Peggy return.'

'And to see me disappear beyond the horizon?'

'Well, she has mentioned it to me.'

'I suppose that devout hope also applied to you?'

'Not exactly.' He frowned, holding her gaze while the question in his eyes seemed to search for an answer to this point. Then, having come to a decision, he murmured, 'Perhaps this will help you to believe otherwise.'

His head lowered as his arms went about her again, holding her even closer than before, and while she again told herself to protest, she found she was without the power to do so. Her pulses were racing, and she became aware of the mounting passion that swept through her as he clasped her body against the length of his own.

But even as his hand found its way to hold her breast in a firm clasp, causing her lips to part helplessly, she knew a sudden panic. His bedroom door was only a few yards away, and he had merely to swing her from her feet and carry her into the seclusion of its four walls just as he had carried her to the bed in the honeymoon suite. And if that happened——

Fear of her own weakness and inability to resist him caused her panic to increase, and it took all her strength to drag her mouth away from his, and to push his hand from her breast as she gasped, 'No, please, Brent, this is too much.'

He looked down at her. 'Are you afraid of me, or of yourself?'

'A little of both, I think,' she admitted.

'At least you're honest. Very well, I can be patient.'

'Patient? Wh-what do you mean?'

'I mean that you're not quite ready and that I can wait.'

Lana stared at him uncertainly, her eyes wide with apprehension. Did he mean what she thought he meant? She feared that he did, and his hands on her shoulders almost made her wince.

'You've been asleep for too long, Lana. It's time you were jerked into wakefulness.' His voice had become husky.

'What are you talking about?'

'The twins told me all I needed to know.'

She felt angry. '*Those two!* how *dare* they discuss me?'

'Their prattling tongues told me enough to make me guess that you're still—untouched. Your body is dormant. It's time it came to life.'

She could only gape at him speechlessly.

His hands dropped from her shoulders. 'OK, I'll find that Rangiatea booklet.' He left her and went to the bookshelf where he began searching but without much success. 'I know it's around somewhere,' he declared, sifting fruitlessly among a pile of magazines.

'If you can't find it now perhaps I could see it tomorrow,' she suggested, still conscious of the effect he had had on her.

'No. I want you to read it this evening because I doubt that you'll have time to do so tomorrow.' Frustrated, he stared at the shelves, then said, 'Perhaps it's among a jumble of periodicals in my bedroom.'

As he left the bookshelves the sound of a tapping on the door came to her ears. It was a knock that was so quiet and discreet it barely registered in her bemused mind, but it was sufficient to jolt her to her senses, and, going to her bedroom door she spoke in a low voice. 'Brent, you have a visitor. Someone is at the door.'

He sent her a casual glance. 'Oh? Please see who it is.'

As she went back towards the door the knocking came again, this time with more persistence, and for some reason she felt reluctant to answer it. Even with her hand on the latch instinct caused her to hesitate, but Brent had said to see who was knocking, therefore she had no option but to do so. Then, taking a deep breath, she opened the door and found herself face to face with Camille.

Green eyes flashed in angry surprise as the older woman stepped into the room, took a swift glance at its emptiness apart from themselves, then turned towards Lana. 'What are you doing in here?' she demanded coldly.

'I'm—just waiting,' Lana informed her quietly.

'Waiting for what, may I ask? I can see that Brent's not here, I can see you're alone.' Then before Lana could speak she rushed on, 'It's also easy to see that you're snooping about in his apartment. You're looking for anything you can pick up.'

The attack shocked Lana. 'Are you suggesting I'm a *thief*?' she demanded furiously. *'How dare you?'*

More angry words came hissing from Camille's thin lips. 'Money, that's what it is. You're looking for money that might be lying around, and when its loss is discovered some other unfortunate member of the staff will be blamed, anyone but the quiet little blonde at the desk. Oh, yes, there's no doubt about still waters running deep!'

The first sounds of the vicious tones had brought Brent to his bedroom door, where he stood listening to Camille, who had her back turned towards him. But Lana could see him and the situation struck her as being humorous. She began to laugh, but her mirth served only to infuriate Camille.

The green eyes flashed with temper. 'You stupid giggling *twit*! Does your bird-brain imagine he'd ever look twice at you? Wait till I tell him about your intrusion into his rooms. Yes, I *do* suggest you're nothing but a common thief, and I'd like to know how you got in here.'

Brent's voice drawled from behind her. 'I let her in. Lana is a guest in my apartment.'

Camille gasped as she swung round to face him. 'Brent! I didn't know you were here.'

'Obviously.' He paused as though waiting for her to say something, but when she continued to stare at him in silence he said, 'Doesn't it occur to you that you owe Lana an apology?'

His hard expression was enough to bring Camille to her senses. 'Oh—yes—of course I do.' She turned to Lana with a forced smile, then gushed effusively, 'My *dear*, I'm so sorry for misjudging the situation, but *naturally* you'll understand that I had Brent's interests at heart. My first thought was to protect his belongings.'

'From my sticky fingers,' Lana snapped furiously, still smarting beneath the sting of Camille's hurtful words.

'My dear, surely you know what members of *any* staff are like,' Camille went on in a confidential tone, and as though this statement lifted Lana to a higher level. 'Few are to be trusted.'

Brent interrupted her coldly. 'You're doing the members

of my staff an injustice, Camille. They've all been with me for years and I have confidence in the honesty of each one of them.'

Camille gave a light laugh. 'If you say so,' she retorted with a superior air, 'but don't moan to me when you find yourself mistaken.' The look she swept over Lana indicated she had had the last word.

Lana was suddenly tired of the situation. She gestured towards the booklet in Brent's hand and said, 'You found what you were searching for?'

'Yes. It'll not take long to read and the illustrations will show you what to look for in the church.'

She took it from him. 'Thank you. I'll study it this evening in bed. Now if you'll excuse me.' And without deigning to glance at Camille she snatched her hat from the chair and left the room.

The sound of the latter's shrill laugh followed her into the passage, but when she reached her room her composure left her and she lay on the bed with one arm flung across her face. Camille's suggestion that she could be a thief had hurt, and now that she thought more about the incident she realised that Brent had said very little to reprimand Camille for her unjust accusation.

Or had he recalled the maxim of least said, soonest mended? And after all, Camille was a guest whereas she herself was merely staff, despite the fact that he had held her in his arms. A quiver ran through her as she remembered the ardour of his kisses and the feel of being pressed against his body. It was enough to wipe away her depression, causing her to spring from the bed and make her way to the staff bathroom where she showered before changing for dinner.

By the time she entered the dining-room Brent and Camille were already seated at their table. Brent stood up, indicating that Lana should join them, but she told Betty to let him know she wished to sit alone. She then took the small table beside the wall, but had hardly sat down when he was beside her.

'You have no wish to sit with us?' he demanded in a low voice, his frown indicating displeasure.

She forced herself to smile sweetly. 'None whatever. Nor do I intend to sit with someone who looks upon me as a thief. It would be enough to give me indigestion.'

'Camille said she was sorry,' Brent reminded her.

Lana continued to smile. 'You'd have to be joking if you imagine I'm convinced on that point.'

'You appear to have made up your mind. OK, I'll see you tomorrow. I've told the Crosbys we'll leave at two o'clock.'

She felt vaguely regretful as she watched him stride back to his table, and then she wondered if he would tell Camille about the pending visit to the church. It was highly probable, and Camille would immediately decide that she must come too. No doubt she had already seen the church a dozen times, but how could she bear to miss another opportunity, especially with Brent at her side?

The thoughts depressed Lana, and suddenly there was no joy left in her anticipation of tomorrow's visit to the church. She had no wish for Camille to accompany them, and she knew that if this happened her own day would be completely ruined.

However, if Brent wanted Camille to come with them there was nothing she could do about it, and suddenly she was horrified to realise that she was bitterly jealous of the red-haired woman. She was jealous of the attention Brent appeared to lavish on her, and of the place Camille seemed to have in his thoughts.

Nor did she wish to see them walking in the moonlit garden, therefore she went to bed early, and as she lay propped against the pillows she examined the booklet entitled *The Rangiatea Story*. The cover illustration showed

the high gable and tall, narrow windows of the church's
eastern facade, with people walking towards the building.
The inner pages told how the church had come into
existence back in the 1840s when missionaries were
bringing Christianity to the Maori people of New Zealand.

Lana became engrossed in the text which told how the
Maori people had walked for miles into the bush north of
where the church was to be erected, and with their
primitive tools had felled giant totara trees. The huge
trunks had been hauled to the nearest river which floated
them down to the sea. They were then guided along the
coast to Otaki where many willing hands had dragged them
ashore, then heaved them over the sandhills to the site of
the church.

She read that one single tree trunk had been selected for
the ridgepole. Forty feet above the ground it rested upon
the tops of three lofty pillars, each one also formed from a
single tree trunk. All were adzed to their finished smooth
state with stone tools. The three pillars were symbolic of
the Trinity, while the ridgepole signified the unity of three
Persons under one Godhead, binding all three together.

A study of the illustrations told her that the ornate
carving on the church's unique furniture had been done
with greenstone tools, and as she examined the intricate
work of the altar, lectern and pulpit she felt grateful for
having been given the opportunity to peruse the booklet
before entering the building. She then thought of the
Crosbys and felt that they also should be given the chance
to read about the church's history before going to see it.

A glance at her watch told her the hour was not yet late,
and, feeling sure that Brent would approve of her action,
she decided to take the booklet to them. They would be easy
to find, either in their room or in the lounge playing cards
with other guests.

She slipped out of bed, dressed hurriedly and made her

way to the lounge. As she had guessed, the Crosbys were playing bridge, and even from the doorway she could see Elmer frowning irritably at the cards he had been dealt.

Claramae took the booklet from her gratefully. 'This is mighty kind of you, my dear. I'll be glad to take a peep at it before we go. Look, Elmer, it's a book about that church we're going to see tomorrow.'

He peered over his glasses. 'Hopefully you'll not begin reading it now. I said one diamond.'

Lana made a hasty retreat, leaving them to go out to the veranda where she stood gazing across the lawn towards the calm sea, dappled by a pathway of sparkling moonlight. Beyond it the length of Kapiti's hump rose darkly, just as it had when the church was being built almost a century and a half ago.

A sigh escaped her as she sensed the romance in the still night air. The tide was out, leaving the sand firm, and she knew it would be pleasant to walk along the beach beside the white frothy wavelets that shone as they tumbled and broke along the shore. But there would be little pleasure in walking alone because nothing was any good unless it was shared, and suddenly she was gripped by an unexpected spasm of loneliness. She needed somebody to walk with her, somebody like Brent.

Almost as if to mock her thoughts the sound of a woman's laugh rang on the night air. She looked about her to discover its source, and the next instant she became aware of two people emerging from the beach track across the lawn. Brent's tall figure was easily recognised, nor was there any doubt about the identity of his female companion. Camille, of course. Had they found romance on the beach? Lana wondered. The question seemed to grip her heart with an icy hand and then, as they drew near, Camille's voice came to her ears.

'Brent dear, that was most exhilarating. Thank you for

refusing to allow me to walk alone. It was just like old times.'

Lana saw the hand that was laid on his arm, and she watched as Camille raised her face to brush his cheek with her lips. Just like old times? What were the old times? Somehow the cold feeling about her heart became more intense. Then, not wishing to hear or see more, she turned away and drew back into the shadows of the veranda.

But Brent saw her as he came up the steps. His voice echoing with surprise, he left Camille and moved towards her. 'Lana, I thought you said you were going to bed early.'

She forced herself to smile at him. 'I did. I read the booklet, then thought the Crosbys should also be given the chance to read it, so I dressed again and took it to them. I hope you don't mind.'

'Of course not. It was the right thing to do,' he approved.

Camille's curiosity got the better of her. 'What booklet is this?' she asked, stifling a yawn.

'Oh, it's just *The Rangiatea Story*,' Brent said casually.

She uttered a short laugh. '*That* old place? I've seen it many times.' Her tone indicated boredom.

Lana looked at Brent, her eyes full of questions. Had he told Camille they would be visiting the church tomorrow? Apparently not, otherwise she would have made clear her intention to join them. So was he about to do so now? Again apparently not, because he remained silent on the subject.

Relieved, at least for the moment, she smiled more warmly as she said goodnight and left them to make her way back to bed. But as she closed her eyes while lying against the pillow she had a mental vision of Camille walking along the sands beside Brent.

Her active imagination saw Camille smiling up into his face, Camille taking his arm, then casually sliding her fingers down it to clasp his hand. Would he pause to turn to face her and take her in his arms? Would he kiss Camille as he had kissed herself only a few hours previously?

The thought agitated Lana to such an extent she sat bolt upright in bed to reprimand herself. Stop torturing yourself, you *idiot*. OK, so you're jealous. What can you do about it? Nothing, absolutely nothing except console yourself with the thought of going out with him tomorrow. And if he decides to take Camille as well, there's still nothing you can do about it.

Good grief, anyone would think you were in love with him, when of course you're *not*. How could you be, when you've known him for such a short time? As for those kisses that turn you into a quivering jelly, you can forget them, because when he's not kissing you he's sure to be kissing Camille, who has only to raise an eyebrow to draw him down to the sands in the moonlight.

OK, have you got the message? *Right*. Then for Pete's sake forget him. She turned and thumped the pillows vigorously, then lay down to stare wide-eyed into the darkness until she drifted off into a sleep that was made restless by irritating dreams.

Hazily, she knew that Peggy had returned from the South Island and was again at the desk. Brent was in the office, but when she tried to speak to him Camille slammed the door in her face. The time of her departure had come and she was packing her bags. She was going away without seeing him again—and suddenly it was a relief to wake up because even if these things came to pass they wouldn't happen today. Peggy was not yet back at the desk, and this afternoon she was going to see the old church with Brent and that nice American couple.

The morning passed rapidly because she was kept busy between the desk and typing letters in the office. Little time was taken over lunch, and then she hurried to her room where she changed into a full-skirted lilac sundress with matching jacket. She took extra care with her make-up, then filled in time at the desk until two o'clock when the Crosbys came to the foyer and Brent drove the white Jaguar to the front entrance.

Claramae Crosby sent appraising eyes over Lana, then spoke to her husband. 'Elmer, isn't she a picture? If I had her complexion, that flaxen hair and those eyes, lilac colour would never leave my back.'

'You do OK, my dear,' Elmer assured her briefly. 'I like your reds and yellows. They're bright, happy colours.'

At that moment Brent came up the steps, his casual short-sleeved navy shirt and well-cut light grey trousers betraying his muscular form and a virility that caused Lana to catch her breath. She became vitally conscious of his magnetic sensuality, and the knowledge that this man had held her in his arms made her feel weak.

She also became aware of a strange stillness about him as he stood regarding her. It was almost a tenseness broken by Claramae's drawl as she exclaimed, 'Isn't she just something to look at?'

Lana felt embarrassed, but it was the sight of Camille coming down the stairs that startled her into action. Smiling at Brent, she said, 'Let's go. Mrs Crosby is keen to see the church.'

They went down the steps, and when Brent opened the car doors he put Elmer Crosby in the front passenger seat while Claramae and Lana sat together at the back. Belts were fastened, and then Lana's spirits sank as she heard Camille's voice call from the veranda.

'Brent, Brent, where are you going? Wait for me, I want to come with you.' She ran down the steps towards the car and rushed to the driver's window. Green eyes flashed over the car's occupants, taking in the seating space between Lana and Claramae Crosby. 'Where are you going?' she demanded again. 'I can see it's one of your guest trips— except that they're not all *guests*.'

But before Brent could answer Claramae leaned forward to speak with unconcealed irritation. 'Young woman, if it's any business of yours, Elmer and I are being taken to see an old Maori church.'

Camille ignored Claramae, her eyes glowing as she spoke to Brent. 'You're going to Otaki? Oh, I'd love to see the old church again. Please take me with you, there's plenty of room in the car.' Her tone had become pleading.

Lana held her breath as she awaited Brent's reply, but Claramae cut in again, this time making less effort to disguise her annoyance. 'I'll have you know there is not plenty of room, and if there's one thing I hate it's to be crushed in a car. I don't want my dress to get all mussed up.'

Camille glared at her, then said pointedly, 'I'm too slim to crush you. You can both move over.'

'It's too hot to have more than four in the car,' Claramae continued to complain snappishly.

Brent revved the motor, then sent Camille a disarming grin. 'I think Mrs Crosby has made herself clear, and in any case you live near enough to the church to visit it whenever you feel like it. Now, if you'll excuse us.'

As the car moved forward Lana glanced through the back window in time to catch a fleeting glimpse of the rage in Camille's eyes. She could also see Brent's face in the rear-vision mirror, the frown on his forehead and the lines about his mouth indicating his displeasure over the incident.

Watching him, she sensed that he simmered with an inner anger, but against whom she was unsure. Was his wrath against Camille for causing their outing to begin on a sour note, or was it against herself for being there instead of Camille? But if this were so, why hadn't he invited Camille insted of her?

Nobody spoke until Elmer Crosby sent Brent an apologetic glance. 'I'm afraid my wife doesn't like that young woman.'

Lana saw his expression become inscrutable, then heard him say, 'Oh? There hasn't been anything really unpleasant, I hope?'

'Not exactly,' Elmer admitted. 'It's just that her lofty attitude gives us both a pain. In my case it's a real bellyache, and she gets under Claramae's skin to such an extent that if she'd come my wife's afternoon would have been ruined.'

Brent said nothing and the subject was not pursued, although Claramae sent Lana a sly glance as her husband's words reached their ears. 'And your day too, I think,' she said quietly.

Lana felt she had to be honest, so she nodded silently.

The road from the beach reached the highway, and within a short time the willow-flanked Waikanae river had been crossed. Almost ten miles further on another bridge took them over the shingled bed of the Otaki river, and as they drove through the small Otaki settlement Claramae told Lana about life at home in the States.

She listened attentively to the older woman, although there were times when Brent caused her mind to wander by catching her eye in the rear-vision mirror. On one occasion he actually smiled at her, giving her the impresson he was now over his former animosity, and the knowledge was enough to lift her spirits. Feeling relaxed, she responded to Claramae's chatter, and within a short time they had reached the road where the church stood beside its headstone-filled cemetery.

As they walked towards the small building Brent explained that the original thatch walls had been replaced by weatherboard, and that this had since been strengthened by buttresses. Totara shingles had also replaced the first thatched rood, and in time these had given way to an iron roof.

When she went inside the church Lana found she could only stand and gaze up at the three lofty pillars. To read about them had been one thing, but to feel and touch their smoothness, to realise that each had been a single tree trunk, filled her with wonder. 'How could they possibly get the ridgepole across the top of them?' she whispered to Brent.

He was standing so close his lips almost brushed her upturned cheek as he bent to speak in her ear. 'There are various theories about that,' he told her in a low voice, 'the most popular one being that many people climbed up a high scaffolding.'

She was too conscious of his nearness, and her voice shook slightly as she asked, 'But the pillars themselves, how were they erected?'

'That, also, is still a matter of conjecture. In those days there were many trees with trunks reaching from sixty to eighty feet before the first branches.' His hand rested on her arm, then slid down its length to clasp her fingers.

The action took her by surprise, but she endeavoured to remain calm as she said, 'The booklet says these pillars are forty feet high.'

'And sunk to a depth of six to eight feet as well.' The pressure on her fingers tightened as he gazed at her upturned face. 'Is it the atmosphere in here that makes you want to whisper?'

She nodded wordlessly, almost afraid to look at him lest her eyes betrayed her inner exhilaration caused by the feel of his fingers entwined about hers.

His voice was still low as he said, 'Come and see the altar table. It's over forty inches wide and formed from a single slab of totara timber.' Without releasing her hand he tucked her arm beneath his own, then drew her towards the semicircular rail that curved across the front of the altar.

Lana's breath quickened as they stood together, his arm

keeping her close to his side, and while she tried to appreciate the ornate carving on the rail, she became conscious of Brent's aftershave, and vitally aware of his physical attraction which forced itself upon her to such an extent she almost felt weak at the knees.

A quick glance over her shoulder showed that the Crosbys were engrossed in gazing up at the crossbatten ceiling, and at the rafters decorated with scroll designs, yet despite their company she felt only Brent's presence. It was almost as if they were alone, especially as he continued to hold her hand.

She also became conscious of a change in his attitude towards her. His suspicions concerning her feelings towards Eric seemed to have disappeared, at least for the moment, and there was a hint of tenderness in his manner that kindled a quiet happiness within her. Something intangible appeared to have sprung up between them, something that made her heart beat so fast it sent the blood racing through her veins.

An invisible magnet caused her to turn and look at him, and she realised he was regarding her intently. But while she tried to read the expression in his eyes, she was unaware of the sparkling glow in her own, or the heightened colour in her cheeks that made her look more beautiful than she herself could have thought possible.

But suddenly the magic moments were shattered as Claramae came to stand beside Brent, a twinkle in her eyes as she looked up into his face and said earnestly, 'Ah, I see you've been smart enough to get this lovely girl to the altar at last. A very wise move, and let me tell you she's a much better choice than that other one.'

The words horrified Lana, throwing her into a state of confusion. She saw the shutter that swept across Brent's face, changing it into an inscrutable mask, and she knew that he had dropped her hand as though it had burnt his fingers. She was also forced to acknowledge that his previous tenderness towards her had merely reflected the serene atmosphere of the church.

Claramae's voice continue as she turned to her husband. 'Elmer, let me see that booklet again. What does it say about all this lattice-work on the walls? Isn't it done with flax, that stuff that grows in the swamps?'

They moved away and somehow managed to take a little of Lana's inner joy with them. She peeped at Brent, fearing that he would now be in an angry frame of mind, but if this was so he gave no sign of it while leading her to examine the intricate carving of the pulpit.

They left a short time later, and as they were about to get into the car for the homeward drive Brent pointed to a monument that had been erected to Te Rauparaha. 'That's the place where the old chief was buried,' he told Lana. 'But within a short time his remains were removed to Kapiti Island. Some day I'll take you over to what was once his stronghold.'

His words lifted her spirits again, but she gave a light laugh that held disbelief. 'Some day? It'll have to be soon. You're forgetting that Peggy will be back and then I'll return to my old job in Wellington.'

Claramae spoke as she climbed into the back seat. 'Who is this Peggy? I've heard her name mentioned but haven't set eyes on her.'

'She's the permanent receptionist,' Lana explained. 'She went to the South Island on the day you arrived. I'm merely a stand-in.' She went on to explain Peggy's necessity to attend her sister's wedding at Bluff in the south of the South Island.

'Well, you do amaze me,' Claramae exclaimed. 'I felt sure you were so very much a part of the place.' She turned to her husband. 'Didn't I, Elmer? Didn't I tell you that this girl is really a part of Leisure Lodge?'

'You sure did say those very words, Claramae,' he agreed, 'but then you're the world's number one matchmaker.' The statement was accompanied by a grin and broad winks directed to Brent and Lana.

His action caused them to laugh, and this relieved the tension in a situation which could have meant further embarrassment for Lana. Nevertheless, during the drive home a few veiled glances in the rear-vision mirror showed that Brent's brow was again darkened by a frown. She noticed that he had little to say, and it dawned upon her that he had not been amused by the well-meaning if misguided remarks that had been bandied about by Claramae Crosby.

Sadly, she realised it meant that he had no wish to be associated emotionally with her, but because the Crosbys were guests he had had no option but to hold his anger in check. It also meant that what she had imagined to be a changed attitude in the church had been no more than wishful thinking on her part, and she was almost glad when the journey was over.

CHAPTER SEVEN

WHEN they reached the guest-house Eric's welcome was almost effusive. 'Thank heavens you're back!' he exclaimed to Lana, his face beaming at the sight of her. 'There are some urgent letters to be answered and unless they're sent at once we'll have double bookings on our hands. If there's one thing that sends Hilary up the wall——'

'It's double bookings,' Lana completed for him. 'Is this the result of a mistake on my part?'

'Not at all,' Eric assured her.

Brent spoke in a cool voice. 'Lana is supposed to be having the afternoon off.'

Eric grinned. 'She won't mind sacrificing it for me.' His tone was full of confidence as he turned several pages of the register, then pointed to a block booking. 'On this date we have a party of senior citizens doing a tour. They want to add a few extras, but there's a limit to our accommodation and we must let them know.' He turned to Lana. 'You don't mind getting back into harness?'

'Of course not.' She was almost afraid to look at Eric because Brent's sharp glances were darting between them. 'However, I intend to have a cup of tea first, so I'll see if the trolley is still in the lounge.'

When she reached the large room with its comfortable chairs the Crosbys were already there, drinking tea and telling their bridge-playing companions of the previous evening about the old Maori church. Hilary was also there, pouring tea for guests, and when she saw Lana the smile she sent did not quite reach her eyes.

'Ah, there you are, Lana,' she exclaimed with an edge to her voice. 'Really, I'm not sure what to do about you. My husband has been moaning—positively *moaning* over your absence.'

Lana looked at her blankly. 'But I've been away for—for only a couple of hours.'

'Don't you see? That's just the point. One would imagine he couldn't possibly do without you.'

The words were lightly spoken, but Lana sensed the underlying resentment in them, so, matching Hilary's light tone, she said, 'Please be assured it's only my typing he needs, not my company.'

'He never goes on in this manner when Peggy has time off,' Hilary continued crossly. 'I'll be glad when that girl returns and we can get back to normal.'

Camille, who had been sitting near by, now stood up and came to the trolley to receive a second cup of tea. 'You found the old church interesting, Lana?' she drawled in a bored voice.

'Yes. It has its own special atmosphere.'

'Why didn't you tell me Brent was taking you to visit it?'

'Because he himself could have told you if he'd wanted to.'

'You could have explained more clearly. I mean last evening when he was lending you that booklet.' Camille's voice had become brittle.

'I didn't see that it was any concern of yours,' Lana smiled.

'I'll bet you didn't. You knew he would have wanted me to go too.'

'Then why didn't he ask you? He had his chance to do so just as we were leaving, remember?'

Camille's green eyes flashed and her voice became raised. 'You know very well it was the fault of that—that stupid American.'

'Stop it, Camille,' Hilary hissed in a low voice. 'If you must quarrel with Lana kindly do it elsewhere. You're making a spectacle of yourself, and it's not the type of entertainment I like to provide for guests. Can't you see people are listening to you?'

Camille took control of herself. 'I'm sorry,' she began, then fell silent as she glanced about the room to meet the eyes of several people who listened with avid interest. Among them was a tight-lipped Claramae Crosby, who had edged closer and looked as if she was about to join in the argument.

Hilary spoke to Camille in a tense voice. 'Personally, I can't see why you should be so uptight because Brent took Lana to see the church. They were away for only a short time.'

Camille gave an exclamation of impatience. Her mouth became a thin line as she gritted from behind clenched teeth, 'You're blind, Hilary. I know you're worried about this girl and Eric, but can't you see she's really setting her sights on Brent? Surely you can understand that *I'm* the one he should have taken. I'm back with him now.'

Hilary's expression betrayed incredulity. 'Are you saying you've taken up wher you left off? I had no idea.'

'Well, I have—almost. So you can believe that going to see that old church is the nearest she'll ever get him to an altar.'

Lana felt it was time to remind Camille of her presence. 'So what are you worrying about?' she asked, forcing herself to smile and remain calm while trying to fathom the exact meaning of the exchange between them.

But Camille ignored her. She put her cup down with a slight bang and left the room.

Hilary shook her head in a bemused manner. 'I must watch myself,' she confessed. 'I must not allow myself to become like Camille. She's burning with jealousy, and when she says you've set your sights on Brent she's really fearing that he might be setting his sights on you.'

Lana frowned. 'I'm afraid I don't understand.'

Hilary lowered her voice. 'I mean I mustn't allow myself to become boiled up with jealousy. When I see Eric gawping at you like a freshly landed fish I must remember it's only because you remind him of his first wife, his—his Ingrid.'

'You can believe it's his only reason,' Lana assured her gravely, then paused before she added, 'Did you ever see a photo of her?'

'Yes, but only briefly. Eric kept one for years, but I advised him to get rid of it. I told him to burn it.'

Lana kept her voice even. 'And he did?'

'I hope so. It only kept the memory of her alive.'

'What about photos of your first husband?' Lana pursued. 'Have you destroyed every photo you possessed of him?'

'Certainly not, but that was different. His death had been more recent, whereas Eric was still clinging to someone he'd lost years ago. I can assure you he's been happier since marrying again.'

'I'm sure you've made him very happy,' Lana said warmly, 'but did you really think that burning the photo would erase the memories he'd had for so many years?'

'At the time I was naïve enough to do so, but now I know that some memories are with us for always. They live with us, and we have to live with them.'

'I believe you're right,' Lana agreed thoughtfully. She knew that the memory of Brent's kisses would remain with her for a long time, and that they would have to be erased from her mind before the caresses of another man could replace them.

When she returned to the office she was surprised by the number of letters to be answered. 'Why should there be this flush of requests for accommodation?' she asked.

'We call it the end-of-season scramble,' Eric explained. 'You'll find they're mainly retired people, and this is the month when they come out in droves. The holiday resorts are no longer teeming with children or with young adults who can't live without loud music, and they imagine they can get quiet places to themselves.'

Lana smiled. 'I can't imagine loud music at Leisure Lodge.'

'It's not that sort of guest-house. We don't need a dance floor or noisy midnight parties to be successful. And I think you can say we are successful,' he added with quiet satisfaction.

She looked at him, unaware that her eyes glowed with admiration. 'Something tells me it's all due to your efforts.'

'Not mine alone. Hilary has also played her part. We've both had years of experience in this sort of management, but thank you for the praise. I think Brent's satisfied.'

'I'm sure he is,' Lana agreed, then fell silent as Brent's words flashed back into her mind. Nothing must stand in the way of the smooth running of the lodge, he had said. Nor could she blame him for being so determined on this point because she now realised that, coupled with the running of the farm, he had a burden of responsibility on his shoulders. It was one that had to be shared by capable people like Eric and Hilary, nor was it any wonder that he feared the possibility of their matrimonial applecart being upset.

Eric's voice came through the haze of her thoughts. 'You're staring at that letter as if you can't read it. Are you having trouble with the handwriting? I know some of them are difficult to decipher.' He left his seat and came to stand behind her, and as he leaned over her shoulder his face remained close to hers.

For one mad moment she was gripped by an almost over-whelming desire to brush his cheek with her lips, to cry aloud, *Don't you recognise me?* But of course he didn't. She was merely a blonde who happened to look like Ingrid. Besides, he'd already rejected her once, and no doubt he would do so again.

Even as she pondered the question a movement caught the corner of her eye and she looked up to see Brent standing in the doorway. The ironic expression on his face gave her a shock, and she feared to guess at the thoughts running through his mind. She also felt her cheeks burn, then become drained of their colour as she thought of the consequences of giving in to her former impulse. Brent's suspicions concerning her feelings towards Eric would have then been confirmed.

She forced her eyes back to the letter she was holding and managed to keep her voice steady as she spoke to Eric. 'I think the name is Braithwaite. Perhaps I can check the address in the phone book.'

'You're having difficulties?' Brent drawled from the doorway. 'There's need to go into a huddle?'

Eric straightened his back, ignoring Brent's hint of intimacy as he reached for the telephone book. 'I wish people would learn to write clearly,' was all he said.

Lana took the book from him and began flicking over the pages. She then ran her finger down the list of names until she was able to pause and say, 'Yes, this is the address in Wadestown.' Then to Brent she added, 'Some handwriting is very difficult to decipher.'

He came into the room, picked up the letter and studied it. 'This doesn't look too difficult to me.'

'It's easy once you've been told what it is,' she retorted, then handed him another which was even more difficult to read than the Braithwaite letter. 'Perhaps you could get to work on that one.'

Brent frowned at the short note. 'Obviously a reservation is required.'

Eric laughed. 'Even we can work out that much, but for whom, and from when to when? We can't read the figures, much less the name.'

Brent's expression became rueful as he returned the letter to Lana.

'OK, point taken. I'm afraid your free afternoon has been nipped in the bud. We'll have to make it up to you in some way.'

'I'll look forward to that, if it ever comes to pass,' she flashed at him, then began to type rapidly.

Eric chuckled. 'Perhaps he'll take you on one of the bush walks where you can help keep an eye on some of the elderly ladies. That'll be a real treat,' he concluded with thinly veiled sarcasm.

'I haven't one arranged at present,' Brent demurred.

'Then arranged one for yourself and Lana,' Eric pursued. 'You might even contrive to become lost,' he suggested, his eyes twinkling as he turned to Lana. 'How would you like to be lost in the bush with Brent?'

She tried to ignore the sly grin on his face. 'It would be an interesting experience,' she said, feeling that something was expected of her. 'However, I don't believe Brent is one who would become lost in the bush.' Nor did she believe she would find herself walking between the dense trees on the foothills with him, feeling the touch of his hand helping her over wet places where streams made the ground slippery.

And that evening at dinner the prospect seemed to be even more remote. Sitting alone at the small table beside the wall she watched Brent move between the tables, chatting amicably to various guests. Camille was with him, oozing grace and charm as she also chatted to people in the manner of the most accomplished hostess.

When they reached the Crosbys' table Claramae's ringing drawl reached Lana's ears. 'Tell me, is there any truth in the rumour that you intend taking over the running of this guesthouse?' she demanded of Camille.

Camille appeared to be startled by the unexpected question but was quick to find an answer. She sent a sidelong glance at Brent, then said boldly, 'Where there's smoke there's usually fire, Mrs Crosby.'

Brent was not amused by their exchange. He frowned at Claramae but asked calmly, 'What would give you such an idea, Mrs Crosby?'

She smiled at him. 'Well, right now she looks as if she's in training for the job, and this afternoon I heard her say she'd—come back.' She turned to Camille. 'Have you been away—*dear*?'

Camille gave a gay laugh, and instead of being affronted by

Claramae's temerity she merely sent another glance towards Brent. 'Yes, I'm back, and one must always be ready to face the inevitable,' she said, as though the inevitable was already settled in her own mind.

Lana then became aware that Betty had paused beside her table with a trolley bearing tempting desserts. 'Did you hear that little lot?' the waitress whispered.

'Who could miss it?' Lana replied, helping herself to trifle and ice cream.

'The big question being, what is the inevitable?' Betty murmured. 'Would you believe there are bets about it going on among the staff? Does she or does she not pin him down this time? We're all noticing that this particular visit is being somewhat extended, and some of us think it's because of you.'

Lana was startled, and her voice became cool. 'Really? How can that possibly be? And you can tell the staff I'm not accustomed to my private life being bandied round as part of a bet!'

'No offence meant, and you might as well become used to it,' Betty grinned impishly. 'You've been part of the wagering about him from the moment you arrived. Besides, he took you out today, didn't he?'

'That was only because time off was due to me.'

'Don't you think Peggy ever had time off due to her? Not once has he ever taken her out. And another thing, some of us have noticed the way he looks at you. I can tell you the staff don't miss much of what's going on in this place.'

Lana's voice remained cool. 'It seems to me that the staff should be commended for their excellent imaginations.'

'Don't you believe it. They can see what's what, all right.'

Lana looked at the waitress apprehensively, waiting for a further comment concerning the fact that Eric had also been seen observing her. But if this was so, Betty failed to mention it.

However, the next outing with Brent came sooner than

expected. In fact it came next morning when she had been at the desk for only a short time, and she turned to find him regarding her from the office doorway. The sight of him caused her heart to flip over, but his words merely gave her a surprise.

'That dress makes you look extremely capable,' he remarked.

She smiled as she looked down at the tailored lines of her deep blue office dress. 'The twins call me Miss Efficiency when I wear it. I put it on because the day is cooler.'

'Or because that particular blue sends depth into your eyes?'

'Are you accusing me of trying to impress somebody?'

'It's possible. No need to mention names.'

'You're quite wrong.' Irritated, she glared at him. Of course he meant Eric.

'I don't intend to argue, Miss Efficiency. I'm more interested in learning how expert you'll be at choosing fruit and vegetables.'

She looked at him blankly, awaiting further explanation.

'I'm taking you to Levin,' he informed her. 'It's a little over twenty miles from here. I intend to visit my accountant, but apart from that I've had an emergency call from the kitchen, and as the place is full of market gardens——'

'I see. Very well, I'll come if you wish.' Or should she have said if you *demand*? There was no suggestion of, would you *like* to come, nor even a, please would you accompany me? It was just a blunt *I'm taking you.* Yet despite these irritating facts she knew she wanted to go with him. 'What about the desk?' she asked, making an effort to hide her eagerness.

'Eric will keep an eye on it. So, shall we go?' Male impatience tinged his voice.

'I'll need to go to my room first,' she said calmly, aware of a bubbling inner excitement as they walked along the staff quarters passageway. This outing with Brent had come so unexpectedly it left her feeling dazed, and as she paused in her room her fingers trembled as she changed into strappy sandals and applied more make-up.

As they crossed the gravelled yard towards the garages she was assailed by a feeling of being watched, and gancing over her shoulder she was not surprised to see faces peering at them from the kitchen windows. Were more bets being laid among the staff?

And then the back door opened as Betty came running across the yard towards them, a slip of paper in her hand. Passing it to Brent, she said, 'Chef would like you to add these items to the list. He's getting low on spices.' She smiled knowingly at Lana. 'Have a lovely day. I must say you look nice. That deep blue dress makes your eyes look like sapphires.'

'Thank you, Betty, it's just colours playing tricks.' A flush rose to Lana's cheeks as she tried to brush the compliment aside. Brent had already accused her of wearing the dress for this very reason, and then the flush deepened as she realised he was regarding her closely.

'You're right, Betty,' he said after a pause. 'Sapphires is the exact word.' He turned abruptly and pushed up the roller door of the garage housing the station wagon. 'We usually take this vehicle when on a vegetable-buying spree,' he explained, opening the car door for her.

She fastened her seat-belt, and as he backed the station wagon out of the garage she turned to send Betty a farewell wave, but the action froze as she found herself greeted by the sight of Camille standing at the back door, obviously questioning the waitress. Then, as the car began to move out of the yard, Camille ran after it, her voice coming faintly through the open windows, *'Brent, Brent, stop. Wait for me!'*

Lana saw him glance in the rear-vision mirror, then realised that although he had seen Camille he was not going to stop. 'That was Camille,' she said. 'I think she wants to come with us.'

'No doubt.' His tone was non-committal and abrupt.

She was relieved by the fact that he had not stopped, yet was unable to resist saying, 'It's a wonder you're not taking her instead of me.'

He stared straight ahead. 'If I'd wanted to take Camille she'd have been sitting beside me instead of you. However, as you can see, it's the other way round.'

She sighed as a thought struck her. 'I dare say you think I'd be better at choosing fruit and vegetables.'

'That's exactly right, Miss Efficiency,' he grinned. 'Now suppose you sit back and try to enjoy yourself. There's no real need to allow thoughts of Camille to nag at your mind.'

'Who says she's nagging at my mind?' Lana protested, even if acknowledging the truth of this to herself.

'I do. Hasn't she driven you from my table in the dining-room?'

'Nobody likes to feel—*de trop*,' she pointed out.

They drove in silence while following the same northern route of the previous day, passing roadside homes where the gardens were bright with the reds, yellows and pinks of tall canna lilies, tiger lilies and marigolds. There were hedges where the white trumpets of convolvulus sprawled to dot the darker green, and as they crossed the Waikanae river bridge Lana's gaze went towards the willows lining the stony bed stretching towards the west.

'So many willow trees,' she said, then added wistfully, 'it must be lovely to walk along the riverbank beneath their shade.'

Brent sent her a swift glance. 'You'd like to do that? There's a track along the bank. We'll take a short walk on the way home.'

She looked at him gratefully, her eyes shining at the prospect. 'Thank you, I'll look forward to it.'

He glanced at the smile playing about her lips. 'That's better. Now I can see you're feeling more relaxed, even happier perhaps.'

'Am I so transparent?' She was indeed feeling happy to be sitting beside him and to know that a state of companionship, even if only temporary, was beginning to build between them. The sight of his handsome profile stirred a sense of satisfaction deep within her, and memory of the feel of his hands, now resting lightly on the wheel, sent a small quiver through her. It caused a tingling sensation of pleasure somewhere near the pit of her stomach, but when she turned to peep at him he was staring straight ahead, apparently engrossed in his own thoughts. Were they about Camille? The fear that this could be so caused her face to become sombre.

'Something's worrying you,' he remarked unexpectedly.

'No, it's nothing of importance,' she assured him, surprised by his observation.

'It appears to have been enough to wipe the smile from your face. Is Camille still sitting on your shoulder?'

Lana decided to be frank. 'Well, yes, she is. I've been puzzled by something that was said yesterday.'

'Oh? Did she poke sticks at you?' His tone was guarded.

'She was talking to Hilary when something was said about taking up where she'd left off. I know it's not my business, but I couldn't help wondering what was meant.'

'It seems clear enough to me.'

'Oh?' She turned to him, her brows arched as she waited expectantly for further explanation.

His shoulders lifted in a small but resigned shrug. 'Sooner or later someone is sure to tell you that Camille and I were once much closer than we are now. It's years ago, and I suppose we were somewhat infatuated with each other.'

'Only—infatuated?'

'Definitely. In any case Camille proved it to be only infatuation on her part. Her father had a farm a few miles from Waikanae, and we had a rendezvous at a half-way place, a secluded spot where we used to meet. One day she phoned to tell me she wouldn't be meeting me on that particular day, or any other day, because she was about to marry somebody else.'

'Oh. That would be Mr Boyd?' There was no bitterness in his voice, she noticed.

'Yes. She'd met Terry Boyd about three months previously. He was a wealthy Australian who'd crossed the Tasman to visit relatives in New Zealand. Needless to say I was a fraction angry at the time.'

'Only a fraction?' Lana looked at him wonderingly.

'I might as well admit I was raving mad when I realised she'd spent three months dating us both. However, her marriage to Boyd didn't last long, because the poor fellow was killed while driving one of his supercharged cars on the Sydney to Melbourne highway.'

'And so Camille came home.'

'Yes, she's back.'

'To take up where she left off,' Lana added, then fell silent while waiting for him to deny that a reunion between them would take place. But when he failed to do so her gloom deepened.

A few miles further along the highway they came upon several roadside stalls that offered a large variety of fruit and vegetables. Brent parked the station wagon before one of the larger colourful displays and together they made their way towards the trays of garden produce.

The stall owner approached Brent. 'Ah, Mr Tremaine, I thought I recognised your vehicle. As it happens, a load of fresh vegetables has just arrived. Come through to the back.'

They followed him to where cases were being unloaded from a lorry. Brent handed the chef's list to Lana, then stood watching while she consulted it and chose carefully. He then left her while he drove the station wagon to the back of the stall, and as the purchases were loaded into the back he examined them with satisfaction. 'You appear to have done this sort of thing before,' he remarked.

The stall owner grinned. 'She knew exactly what to pick up and what to leave. I'd keep her on if I were you,' he added, obviously assuming Lana to be a member of Brent's staff.

'I might do that,' Brent returned gravely, but without looking at Lana.

She sent him an oblique glance as she got into the car. 'Aren't you forgetting that I'm only temporary staff? And very temporary for that matter, because Peggy's holiday is drawing to a close.'

'Is that something I'm likely to forget?' he asked quietly.

'There's no need to hide your relief over the fact,' she remarked lightly, remembering he would be glad to have her out of Eric's sight. Then feeling that a change of subject would be wise, she asked, 'Do you always drive this distance to buy fruit and vegetables?'

He laughed. 'Of course not. There are plenty of places nearer to home where the fertile soil grows produce to feed Wellington, but when I visit my accountant at Levin I usually make purchases at that particular roadside stall.'

The remaining miles slid by as they drove beyond Otaki and through green farmlands until they reached a long stretch of industrial area on the outskirts of Levin. At the end of it lay the shopping-centre, the business premises being tree-sheltered from the heat of the sun.

Brent parked the station wagon beneath the leafy shade of a plane tree, and after making the extra purchases on the chef's list he guided Lana to a restaurant where he ordered a lunch of Canadian red sockeye salmon, salad, wheatmeal bread and coffee.

Sitting opposite him she became vitally aware of his dark eyes raking her fetures until they caught and held her gaze. The almost hypnotic force behind them made her suspect they were trying to penetrate her thoughts, while the slight frown on his brow warned her to expect questions.

At last he said, 'I must admit you're still a puzzle to me,

Lana.'

Her gaze became direct. 'There's nothing very complex about me.'

'I'm not so sure. You are indeed Miss Efficiency, yet you don't appear to be doing anything concrete about your personal life.'

She was lost for words until she said defensively, 'How can you possibly tell what I'm doing with my—my personal life?'

'I can tell it's without an objective because the important signs are missing.'

'You're speaking in riddles. What sort of signs?'

'The mating signs. I haven't noticed any young males rushing to discover why you're spending so much time at Leisure Lodge.'

'That's a sign?' She looked at him incredulously.

'It's one that indicates you're not engaged or even more than friendly with anyone in particular.'

She straightened her back and sent him a direct stare. 'I still don't know why I baffle you. What, exactly, are you trying to say?'

He hesitated, frowning, until he said, 'Well, to be frank, on the one hand you're such a sensible girl, yet on the other hand you appear to have set your sights on a man who's more than twice your age.' The words trailed away as he fell silent.

'I presume you mean Eric.' The food seemed to be going round in her mouth, causing her to find difficulty in swallowing it.

'Of course. Who else could I possible mean at the moment?'

She placed her fork on the plate. 'Must you spoil my day in this manner? Haven't I tried to assure you there's nothing between Eric and me, at least not the romantic association you appear to have conjured up in your own mind?'

'Yes, you have tried.'

'Then please believe it. And let me assure you on another point, you're not half as observant as you imagine yourself to be.' She fell silent, annoyed with herself for having uttered those words, but exasperation had forced them from her.

Brent's eyes narrowed slightly. 'What do you mean?'

She stared at her plate. 'Nothing. It was a silly remark to make.'

'Then why make it?' he asked softly.

'Because you're upsetting me,' she retorted.

'Then simmer down and finish your meal,' he advised.

'I'll try, but you've made me feel I can't eat it.'

'Nonsense. Just drink this.' He poured more coffee.

She made an effort to finish her meal and by the time she had drunk her coffee she felt more cheerful.

He looked at her critically. 'That's better. I believe you're ready to smile again. Something tells me you're not one who indulges in long hours of sulky silence.'

'Even if I were, your remarks are too far from the truth to be worth worrying about,' she informed him loftily.

'I'm glad of that,' he returned, his tone serious. 'However, I'm still curious about your remark concerning my lack of observation. It's unlike you to say such a thing without reason.' He paused thoughtfully, then asked, 'You still refuse to tell me?'

'Definitely, so please forget it.'

'I've a strong feeling I'm missing out on some vital point. Really, Lana, I could happily bang your head against one of those plane trees in the main street!'

'That would make an interesting news item. I can almost see the headlines: Lord of Leisure Lodge knocks sense into lowly receptionist.'

They both laughed as they stood up to leave the table and she felt she had steered his thoughts away from the subject of her former careless remark. Nor did he pursue the matter when they reached the pavement, where he said, 'Do you think you can fill in an hour while I visit my accountant?'

'Easily. I'll browse in the shops. I'd like to find a gift for my mother and perhaps something for the twins.'

'Very well. I'll see you back at the car in an hour's time.'

She tood watching as his tall figure crossed the road, then made its way towards a block of offices. A sudden depression descended upon her, causing her to feel lost without his company, and despite the fact that there were people all round her, walking along the sheltered pavement or standing in groups, she felt very much alone. *Idiot,* she snapped at herself. Anyone would think his presence meant the earth to you, and that, of course, is the height of stupidity.

She squared her shoulders and took several deep breaths in an effort to clear him from her mind, then began to examine the shop windows in her search for gifts. The twins were easy. Necklaces with matching earrings always pleased them, but Mother was a real problem because she seemed to have everything.

And Father—surely he deserved to be remembered by a small gift of some sort. He hadn't turned his back on her when she had been a baby. He had cradled her in his arms and had given her a home. Then, in a flash of fairness, she recalled Eric saying that he had left for England soon after his bereavement, so how could he have coped with her own small self?

Her eyes misted with tears of gratitude as her thoughts returned to John Glenny who had never failed to open his wallet when she had been in need of some item. Ah, that was it, a new wallet would be ideal, because his present one had become worn and shabby.

Inspiration struck again when she stared at the shelves in a shop where prefumes were sold. Did Mother ever buy perfume for herself? The idea was almost laughable, because any spare cash she had was always spent on necessities, or on something for the twins who were not yet earning for themselves.

The search for the gifts caused the time to pass rapidly, and although Lana had finished her shopping well within the hour she almost ran back to where the station wagon was parked.

She told herself she had no wish to keep Brent waiting, but a sudden burst of honesty forced her to admit she longed to be with him again.

CHAPTER EIGHT

WHEN Lana reached the car she was surprised to find Brent sitting in the driver's seat, waiting for her. He got out and opened the door for her, then asked, 'You've had a successful shopping spree?'

'I hope so. They're just small gifts.' She got into the car and unwrapped a parcel. 'Do you think my father will like this wallet? Is it a suitable type?'

He fingered its smooth texture. 'It's genuine calfskin. I'm sure he'll be pleased with it.' He examined and approved her other purchases, then asked, 'What did you buy for yourself?'

She was surprised by the question, her brows rising as she turned to regard him. 'Myself? Nothing. I seldom buy for myself unless there's something I need. What makes you imagine I'd be buying for myself?'

'I thought it was the usual feminine procedure. I know one person who never fails to buy a gift for herself. Jingle-jangles to decorate her arms or hang from her ears.'

'No doubt you're thinking of Camille,' she flashed at him, suddenly irritated. 'As it happens, I am *not* Camille.'

'No, I can see that for myself.' He smiled as though amused.

She rushed on, 'And I can see she's obviously on your mind, constantly sitting in your thoughts. Why don't you marry her and put everyone's mind at rest—especially the kitchen staff who are betting on the result?' She stopped, appalled by her own lack of discretion.

Brent chuckled. 'Don't worry, I know there's speculation in that quarter.'

'Well, why don't you?' she felt compelled to pursue it.

'For two very good reasons,' he returned seriously.

134

'Two reasons?' She looked at him expectantly, then said, 'I'm sorry, I've no right to pry into your private affairs.'

But he continued as if she had not spoken. 'The first reason is the obvious one. I'm not in love with her.'

'But you were once.'

'I told you it was infatuation.'

She looked away into the distance, wondering why she was conscious of such an overwhelming relief. 'And the second reason?' she forced herself to ask.

'I don't believe that Leisure Lodge has room for both Hilary and Camille, at least, not on a permanent basis. I don't think it would work, especially after Camille's transition from guest to boss's wife.'

Lana gave a short laugh. 'I see. It's as you said before, nothing must interfere with the smooth running of the guest-house, not even your own emotional situation.'

He ignored the irony in her voice. 'Sooner or later there'd be a heap of trouble. Haven't you noticed there are times when they have to force themselves to be polite to each other?'

'Yes, there have been times when I thought I sensed tension, but I was never positive about it.' She fell silent, wondering if she should voice the thought simmering in her mind, then, unable to resist it, she asked, 'Suppose you *do* fall in love with Camille, how will you cope with the problem?'

His short, mirthless laugh was almost a snort of derision. 'That state of affairs is most unlikely to arise.'

'But—surely it's not *impossible*?'

'It's quite impossible!' he almost snarled, making no effort to hide his irritation. 'Now, may we change the subject?' He turned the ignition key, shot away from the kerbside and began to drive south along the main highway.

Lana took the hint and pushed Camille from her thoughts while she looked forward to reaching the Waikanae river. Would he remember his promise to walk along the bank? Or had the recent discussion put him into a frame of mind that would cause him to race across the bridge and on towards home? She held her breath as they drove past the Waikanae shopping-centre, then a sigh of relief escaped her as he reduced speed on the bridge before swinging into a parking-bay beneath lofty trees on its southern side.

He looked down at her strappy sandals. 'Are those suitable shoes for walking along a riverbank?'

She shook her head, then admitted ruefully, 'Not really, but with luck they'll not come to much harm.'

'We'll not go far,' he said as they got out of the station wagon, then he gripped her hand to help her down a bank that gave access to the riverbank. Her high heels made walking over the stones difficult, but within minutes they were on a track that twisted between scrubby undergrowth thriving beneath the willow trees.

The path was strewn with stones and protruding roots, and at times her sandals caused her to stumble. On one occasion she pitched forward, then uttered a shaky word of thanks as he caught and held her against him. The action caused her heart to flutter, although she found herself released almost immediately, yet not before she had caught the gleam of a question in his eyes.

'Perhaps I should carry you,' he suggested casually.

'That won't be necessary, thank you, but you're right about my shoes being unsuitable.'

They continued without speaking, the silence being broken only by the song of birds and the burble of water rushing over a stony bed. And then the winding track led into a thick maze of slim willow trunks and foliage-laden branches from which there appeared to be no outlet.

Brent examined the blockage and said, 'Winter floods have sent piles of young saplings against these older trees. They've taken root and are now growing bunched together to end the track.'

Lana was disappointed. 'Can't we get round them in some

way?'

'Only if we scramble up a steep bank on one side, or wade through water on the other side. I'm afraid we can go no further.'

But instead of making a move to retrace his steps he put his arm about her waist while he drew her deeper into the leafy thicket that concealed them from prying eyes. His hands on her shoulders turned her to face him, then his arms drew her closer while his chin rested against the top of her head.

They stood for several minutes without speaking, then a tremor passed through her as she felt his lips brush softly across her forehead in a caress that was almost imperceptible.

'Relax,' he murmured softly, his hand beneath her chin raising her face as his head bent slowly.

She drew a deep sigh of contentment as his mouth covered her own. It was the third time he had kissed her, and secretly she had been aching for it to happen again, although only now did she freely admit this to herself. Her lips parted while her arms crept about his shoulders, her fingers entwining in the hair at the nape of his neck, then fondling the lobe of his ear.

His kiss became rapturous with sensual demands that called for her response to the needs of his body, nor did he make any attempt to conceal the intensity of his arousal. And as one hand found its way to her breast the taut nipple betrayed her yearning to be closer to him, the gentle stroking of his thumb causing spasms of desire that made her feel dizzy, and suddenly she knew she must not lose her head.

His lips left hers while he paused to stare at her, his dark eyes seeming to burn in a face that had now become pale. 'Lana, Lana.' The words came as a husky groan as his mouth found hers again, and his arms held her even closer.

Above their heads the leaves rustled gently while across the dry width of the main riverbed the water sang on its way to the Tasman Sea. The low cliffs stretching along the banks seemed to enclose them in a secluded world of their own, and then his voice came with deep urgency. 'Lana, I want you.'

She felt his hands slide down to her hips to clasp her buttocks and drag her against him, and she heard the demand in his voice. His meaning pierced her brain, causing her to draw a deep breath that was almost a sob as she gasped, 'Now? Oh no——'

'Why not? I know you want me as much as I want you. Let me bring you to life.'

She looked at him dumbly, unable to explain that when she gave herself to a man, for the first time, it would not be during a brief interval on the riverbank, and at a clinical request that was entirely lacking in any words of love.

Brent frowned at her, then repeated, 'Why not? Do you deny that you want me, that you're longing——?'

Shaking her head, she raked about in her mind but could find no more to say than, 'I'm sorry, I can't, not just here and now.'

'OK, so now is neither the time nor the place.' His hands moved to her shoulders, almost shaking her. 'Does this mean you're really hoping and waiting for Eric?'

She wrenched herself away from his grip, her face turning pale with anger. 'How dare you make such a suggestion? It's—it's quite *despicable*.' Please take me home.' Tears blurred her eyes as she turned and stumbled along the path, but the heels of her sandals were too high for making speed over its uneven surface. And then a protruding root caught her toe, causing a cry of pain to escape her as she fell sprawling in the dry dusty ground.

For several moments she lay sobbing, but he was beside her in an instant, his arms lifting her from the river silt. 'Are you hurt?' he asked gently, holding her against him once more.

She stood submissively while he used his clean breast-pocket handkerchief to wipe the tears from her cheeks. '*Yes*, I am hurt. My entire lovely day has been ruined. I wish we hadn't come here.'

'Bad as all that, is it?' he mocked.

'Yes, it is. My knee is grazed, my nylons are ruined, my toe hurts and my pride has been dragged in the dust by your suggestion that I'm just waiting to make love with Eric. I—I feel completely degraded!' She leaned against his shoulder while fresh tears fell.

'And just look at your dress,' he said, ignoring her last remark. 'Deep blue isn't the colour to be worn when rolling in the dirt.' He brushed her skirt with his hand, but the dusty patches refused to be moved from the fabric.

A feeling of hysteria gripped her, causing her to giggle, then she gasped as he swung her from her feet; but before she could protest he was striding along the track. Nor did she really want to protest. The strength of his arms gave her a feeling of security, and she found herself relaxing to the extent of nestling her head against his shoulder. Nevertheless she murmured, 'This is ridiculous. I can walk quite easily.'

'You'll walk when the path is more suitable for those silly sandals,' he retorted as he strode between the willows and bushes bordering the narrow track.

'How was I to know I'd be taken to such a place as this?' she asked in a plaintive voice, while remembering her main aim had been to look nice to go out with him.

Driving home a short time later she saw little of the passing farmlands, the green hills rising on their left or even the road ahead. Instead, she sat in a daze of deep thought, reliving the incidents on the riverbank when he had held her so closely.

She knew their longing had been mutual, but honesty compelled her to admit that the situation had hinged upon those three little words which would have told her he loved her. They would have assured her that those moments had been more than a brief flash of passion soon to be forgotten, but they had not been uttered.

If Brent had told her he loved her, heaven alone knew how helpless and weak she would have become, and suddenly she realised she longed to hear those words more than anything else he could say. A sense of shock came with the knowledge, and while she fought mentally to push it away from her, it became an explosion of truth that could not be denied.

At the same time she refused to admit she was in love with him. It was infatuation, nothing more and nothing less, she assured her own doubting mind. She had been whirled off her feet by this devastating man who had the temerity to place her on the bed in the honeymoon suite, who had kissed her in his apartment, and who had been ready to make love beneath the willows on the riverbank.

Lack of sophistication was her trouble, she decided. She was not used to men of Brent Tremaine's calibre. She was not in the habit of being taken by storm, and when the tempest arrived she was unable to cope with it emotionally. No, she was *not* in love with him. At least she didn't think so. *Or was she?*

When they reached home the car was driven into the yard and parked near the back door. Kitchen staff came out to unload the purchases of fruit and vegetables, and Lana became acutely conscious of the unobtrusive glances that flicked from Brent to herself. She felt rather than saw the sly observation, the searching for evidence telling that perhaps they were now closer to each other than when they had driven away earlier in the day.

Their watchfulness made her doubly careful to keep her eyes away from the man who had held her against his breast, and who had kissed her with such demanding passion. And after making sure that the chef approved of the produce she had chosen she disappeared inside and went to her room, where a change into fresh nylons and a different dress did much to restore her to normal.

And as she examined the discarded deep blue garment she knew it would need to be washed before it could be worn again, so she carried it to the laundry. Warm suds were put into the washtub, the dress was immersed, and she was searching for the soiled patches when Camille spoke from behind her.

The few undies in Camille's hand indicated her purpose in being there, and her surprise at discovering Lana was betrayed when she said, 'You're home very early. We didn't expect you for hours.'

Lana turned to regard her. 'We?'

'Well, Hilary and I. She was sure Brent would keep you out of Eric's sight for hours and hours.' A brittle laugh accompanied her last words.

Lana stared at her as the meaning of them began to register. A cold feeling gripped her, but she managed to say calmly, 'What on earth are you talking about?'

Camille's lip curled. 'I presume you do realise that Brent's sole purpose in taking you was to get you away from under Eric's nose?'

The chill creeping over Lana began to intensify, seeping into her blood until it reached her bones. Could this possibly be true? Had Eric been the only reason Brent had taken her to Levin? What a fool she had been to believe his story about hoping she had the ability to choose fruit and vegetables! And the walk along the riverbank, had that been merely a ploy towards gaining satisfaction fo his own sexual needs? The thought made her cringe.

The iciness in Lana's soul began to deepen and she longed to weep. But she also knew that Camille was regarding her steadily, waiting for a reaction to her words, so she forced herself to appear unruffled. 'Really, Camille, you do get the strangest ideas,' she managed to say calmly, 'although I can understand your disappointment in not being asked to come with us.'

Camille's lips thinned. 'Disappointment? What rubbish! Who cares about going to Levin? I can go there any time I like.'

Lana forced a smile. 'We both know that when the car was leaving you shouted to Brent, but he just drove straight on. However, I can't see that it's sufficient reason to vent your anger on me.'

The green eyes glittered maliciously. 'You don't seem to understand that I'm telling you the bare facts. And it might interest you to learn that Hilary says she intends writing to Peggy to demand her return to work at once.'

Lana was appalled. 'I don't believe you. Hilary wouldn't drag Peggy back before she's due to return.'

'Wouldn't she? You just wait and see for yourself. She's getting really fed up with the situation, and after all, Brent can't be continually taking you out to get you away from beneath Eric's nose.'

'Why not?' Lana was prompted to ask casually. 'Isn't it possible that Brent might like taking me out?'

'Don't fool yourself,' Camille declared loftily.

Lana made no attempt to answer her. She pulled the washtub plug, then replaced the water to give the dress a final rinse.

Watching her, Camille's eyes narrowed with sudden interest, and then the questions came sharply. 'Isn't that the dress you wore to Levin? Why did it need to be washed?'

'It became soiled while we were down on the riverbank,' Lana said casually. 'The ground was so dry and dusty, some of it clung to my dress,' she added with a degree of innocence.

Camille glared at her. 'Riverbank? Which riverbank was this?'

'The Waikanae. We walked where the track runs between the willows.

'I *know* where the track runs,' Camille declared with barely controlled fury. 'Are you saying Brent took you there?'

'Of course. Who else would take me there?'

'I suppose you know that Brent and I——' Baffled anger shook the words which faded abruptly, almost as though she feared she was about to say too much.

Lana turned to stare at Camille. 'You and Brent? Ah, that was your rendezvous years ago?'

Camille's eyes widened. 'Did he tell you that?'

'No. It's your attitude that tells me the place had meaning for you, so it's easy enough to guess it's where you used to meet before you went away to marry someone else.'

'How do you know we had a meeting place?'

'Surely it was common knowledge?'

'Somebody must have told you,' Camille persisted. 'Who was it?'

Lana shrugged. 'Does it matter? The point is that people remember these things just as they remember you went away.'

'Well, I'm back now, and I'll thank you to understand what that means.' Camille's tone was menacing.

'How long is it since you—let him down?' Lana asked.

'Five years, and I'll have you know I did not let him down. We were not officially engaged, nor could I help falling in love with somebody else.'

'Five years,' mused Lana. 'A lot of water has passed down the Waikanae river during that period. What makes you think you'll be able to—to take up where you left off?'

'Because I know Brent. He's a one-woman type of man. He'll come back to me like a homing pigeon. Why do you think I'm always put at his table?' Camille asked smugly.

'Possibly it's because you're such old friends,' Lana suggested. At the same time she felt she had heard enough. Her fingers shook slightly as she placed a hanger inside the shoulders of the dress, and her eyes blurred as she went out to the clothes-line. Why had Brent taken her down to the riverbank? Despite his assertion of not being in love with Camille, had he been merely testing his memories and his emotions concerning their former relationship? And had she herself been a tool to be used in this test? Forget him, you fool, she advised herself, then sighed with exasperation as she realised that, for her, he would be completely unforgettable.

A few days later Lana was at the desk when the phone rang.
She lifted the receiver. 'Good morning, this is Leisure Lodge.'

Raewyn's voice came over the line. 'Is that you, Lana? For
Pete's sake, you sound as if you own the place!'

Lana laughed. 'I haven't quite reached that happy state.'

'Do you reckon you're on the way?'

'Don't be silly.' She felt a sudden anxiety. 'Why are you
ringing? Is everything all right? Mother's OK?'

'No, she's quite ill.'

'*Ill? Mother?*' Panic rose within Lana's breast. Eunice was
never ill. 'What's the matter with her?' she asked at last.

There was a giggle at the other end. 'She's
dying—absolutely *dying* with curiosity!'

Lana became impatient. 'What are you talking about?'

'She's curious about you, of course. You haven't rung or
written, and she's longing to know all about *you know who*.'

'Oh.' She meant Eric, of course.

Raewyn said, 'So we're coming out for lunch. You won't
have to pay for us because Mother's coming too. She's decided
to have a look at him.'

Lana's panic rose again, this time for a different reason. 'I
hope I can rely on discretion from the three of you.'

'Of course,' Raewyn assured her. 'You know Mother, you
can rely on her silence. She's the soul of discretion unless she
becomes really upset, and then she's inclined to blab a bit.'

'I'm not at all worried about Mother's discretion,' Lana said
pointedly. 'It's the yacking tongues of two other people that
are inclined to get me on edge. No need to mention names.'

But her remarks were going unheeded because a discussion
appeared to have arisen at the other end of the line. She
suspected that the receiver was being grabbed from Raewyn,
and after a few diffused sounds of argument Bronwyn's voice
came over the phone. 'Hi there, is that you, Lana? It's me,

Bronwyn. Can you hear me?'

'Only too well,' Lana returned drily.

'Good. Then make sure you tell Brent we're coming. Tell him we'll be wanting to ride the horses this afternoon.' Bronwyn's voice rang with the command usually echoed by Raewyn.

Lana laughed, then said with exaggerated politeness, 'Is that a fact? Then I'm afraid I must regretfully inform you that the horses are all occupied this afternoon. There are only four of them and they're booked for house guests.'

Her bantering tone obviously annoyed Bronwyn, who sounded even more like Raewyn as she said, 'Then you'll have to do something about it. You can tell those people that we're coming from Wellington and will need the horses in the early part of the afternoon. They can use them later.'

'You've got to be joking,' snapped Lana. 'The times are already arranged. Lord help us, who do you think you are?'

'We know who we are,' Bronwyn returned with dignity. 'Nor do we expect them for free. Mother will pay for our rides.'

'You don't seem to understand,' Lana said wearily. 'I've told you, the times are already arranged.'

'And you don't seem to understand that if you don't do something about it I might feel inclined to drop a hint of you know what to you know whom,' Bronwyn threatened smoothly.

Lana made no reply, remaining still while the younger girl's words sent a chill through her. She became aware of an altercation taking place at the other end, and then it seemed that Raewyn had snatched the receiver from Bronwyn.

'Don't worry, Lana,' Raewyn said. 'She won't say a word. I'll kill her if she does.'

And with that promise Lana had to be content, although she was unable to rid herself of a feeling of unease where Bronwyn's babbling tongue was concerned.

It was almost noon when they arrived. The twins, wearing jeans, ran up the front steps closely followed by Eunice, who carried her needlework bag just in case she found an opportunity to do a few stitches.

Bronwyn's eyes darted from left to right. 'Where is he?' she demanded breathlessly.

'I presume you mean Eric,' Lana said coldly.

'No, silly, I mean Brent, of course. Did you tell him about the horses?' the younger girl insisted.

'Certainly not,' Lana snapped, then turned to Eunice. 'Mother, we need to talk. I'll take you to my room where you can all leave your swimsuits or whatever.'

'We haven't come here to swim, we've come to ride,' Bronwyn reminded her.

Lana ignored the remark as she led them along the passage to the staff quarters. She ushered them into her room, and when she had closed the door she turned to face Eunice. 'Mother, you know I'm not in the habit of telling tales, but this time I need your help.' She went on to explain the problem of the horses and Bronwyn's threat to drop hints to Eric.

Eunice was horrified. 'That's blackmail!' she exclaimed, then swung round to face Bronwyn. 'Is this true?'

Bronwyn's face went pink. 'I was only joking,' she said sulkily. 'Lana never could take a joke. She's far too serious.'

'Is she indeed?' snapped Eunice. 'Then let me warn you that I'm also serious, especially when I say that if it comes to my ears that you've said one word out of place your allowance will be stopped for six months, and that goes for Raewyn too.' She paused to draw breath as she glared from one twin to the other.

Raewyn gasped. 'Oh, but that's not fair!'

'Isn't it? Your activities are usually planned together,' her mother declared knowledgeably.

Raewyn turned on Bronwyn. 'I said you were being stupid!' she almost shouted in a fury. 'From now on you'll remember that we do what *I* say. Your plans always go haywire.'

'I've got to have a say in what we do,' Bronwyn protested.

Eunice intervened. 'Be quiet, girls, that's enough on the subject, but remember you've been warned. Now then, Lana, when am I going to meet this—this Mr Halversen?

Eric was in the office when they returned to the desk, and at Lana's request he came out to be introduced to Eunice and the girls. The latter, she was relieved to note, refrained from giggling, possibly because they realised that giggling would rank with words spoken out of place and could cause them great financial loss. Their allowances had been cut on previous occasions, Lana recalled. It had been most effective.

Eric's blue eyes twinkled as he shook hands with Eunice. 'I can see you're the mother of the twins,' he remarked affably, 'but Lana must take after her father.'

'Yes, she is rather like her father,' Eunice admitted faintly, her eyes on Eric's flaxen hair.

Lana noticed the twins send swift glances towards each other, and watching them narrowly, she guessed that their amusement lay perilously near the surface. It was a relief when they decided to go outside and sit at one of the lawn tables before lunch.

A few minutes later Hilary came to the desk. She was introduced to Eunice, then said politely, 'Lana has been a tremendous help to us. It was kind of her to sacrifice her holiday to help us when we became short-handed. We haven't anyone else on the staff who could have taken over the desk in such a capable manner.'

'She's been a tower of strength,' Eric added with enthusiasm, 'and she's very much more efficient than Peggy, the girl who's normally here. To be honest, I've enjoyed having her around.'

Hilary sent him a long thoughtful look, then turned to Eunice. 'You might as well know the truth, Mrs Glenny. My husband has taken a very strong fancy to your daughter. He seems to be really drawn to her.'

Startled, Eunice appeared to search for words. 'Oh, well, I don't suppose it's so very surprising, because—after all——' She drew a deep breath, swallowed hastily, then fell silent.

Hilary looked at her with interest. 'Yes? Because?'

'Because, well, because everyone loves Lana,' Eunice finished lamely, then added quickly, 'I'm glad she's been able to help. I've tried to teach the three girls to do all they can to help other people, and while it's been an uphill job with the twins, it's always seemed natural for Lana to hold out a helping hand.'

Lana smiled faintly. 'In this case it's been no trouble at all.'

'How long are you to be here?' Eunice pursued. 'When is this other girl, Peggy, coming back to her job?'

'She's not due before the end of next week,' Lana told her, 'but I understand she'll be back much earlier.'

Eric was surprised. 'What gives you that idea?'

'Camille told me that Hilary intended writing to demand her return!' Camille's words had continued to niggle at Lana, and impulsively she now snatched at the opportunity to straighten the matter in her mind.

Hilary flushed as she avoided Eric's eye. 'Camille had no right to make such a statement,' she said with an edge to her voice.

'What is this?' Eric demanded of Hilary. 'Why would you write to ask Peggy to come back before her holiday had ended?'

Hilary became slightly agitated. 'I didn't write to her, but it was Camille's idea that I should. She's anxious to see Lana away from this place, her reason being more than obvious, especially where Brent is concerned. However, you know perfectly well that the situation has now changed, because Peggy will not be returning.'

Lana was amazed. 'Not be returning?' she echoed.

'There was a letter from her in this morning's mail,' Hilary said. 'Her mother is ill and she can't leave home. Now then, Eric will take you in for lunch while I remain at the desk. The dining-room is fairly full, so he'll take you to our table.'

'Thank you,' Lana murmured. She felt dazed by the news that Peggy would not be coming back to Leisure Lodge, but she gave no sign of it as she went to the door and called to the twins.

They came at once and as they entered the foyer Hilary favoured them with one of the smiles she usually reserved for guests. 'Hello, girls, I see you've decided to pay us another visit.'

Raewyn answered in her most polite manner. 'Oh, yes, we've been longing to come back. The last time was marvellous, and we've wanted our mother to see the place.'

Bronwyn slid a defiant glance at Lana, then spoke to Hilary. 'Are the horses all booked for this afternoon, Mrs Halversen?'

Hilary consulted a book on the desk. 'Yes, I'm afraid they are. Sorry about that.'

'Oh, well, next time perhaps,' sighed Bronwyn, avoiding Lana's eyes, but whispering to Raewyn, 'At least it was a try.'

When they went into the dining-room a quick glance towards the corner table showed Camille to be already seated at it, but of Brent there was no sign. And while Lana longed to ask Eric if he would be in for lunch she found herself unable to voice the question.

But Raewyn saw no need for hesitation. She dimpled at Eric and asked, 'Where's Brent?'

'I think he's busy with the farm manager,' Eric told her. 'Have you a particular reason for wanting to see him?'

'Yes, we want Mother to meet him,' Raewyn replied seriously.

Her words caused Lana to send Raewyn an enquiring look, and as they seated themselves at Eric's table she wondered why the younger girl thought this should be important. Nor had she any intention of admitting that she also was anxious for her mother to meet Brent. In some strange way it had now become imperative for her to know that they approved of each other. In fact it had become more essential for Mother to like Brent than it was for Eric to meet with her approval.

In the meantime Eric had placed Eunice on his right and Lana on his left. He looked at the twins apologetically as he said, 'A table meant for four can mean a crush. Would one of you like to sit at Brent's table?'

They both moved with alacrity. 'We don't mind at all,' Raewyn assured him with a happy smile.

'I meant only one of you,' Eric protested.

'We always do things together,' Bronwyn told him.

Eric then introduced Eunice and the girls to Camille, who favoured them with cool appraisal. Nor was Camille amused when he pushed their tables closer together so that they almost formed one party. The glare she sent him brimmed with resentment, and then she did her utmost to ignore the twins who were already engaged in lowered conversation.

Watching them, Lana guessed they were planning their attack on Brent with regard to the horses. Possibly it would be the poor little city girls deprived of country joys approach, or it might be sorrowful accusations of you *know* you *promised* that the next time we came——

At one time their determined tactics would have annoyed her, but now she merely smiled as she watched their serious expressions. And it was then she realised that she herself had matured since coming to Leisure Lodge, perhaps because she had fallen in love. This fact she now freely admitted to herself, although she also realised that dreaming of Brent was a pointless exercise.

CHAPTER NINE

THE sound of an excited giggle from the twins indicated that Brent had come into the dining-room, and, as she watched him, Lana's heart beat a little faster as he made his way between the tables. His progress was slow because he paused to speak to various guests, and even to say a kindly word to the kitchen staff member who served as an extra waitress when the dining-room became busy.

On reaching Eric's table he was introduced to Eunice, and although the flicker of surprise in his eyes was only momentary, it did not escape Lana's observation. She knew a sudden fear that he might begin to question why there was so little mother-and-daughter resemblance between them, and while she had been happy to see Eunice, she found herself wishing the trio had stayed away.

However, it was easy to guess that the visit had been arranged by the twins who had worked on their mother's curiosity as an excuse to return, and as Brent pulled out his chair to sit down their round faces beamed at him.

Raewyn's voice rang clearly. 'Mother was longing to see where Lana was working, so we decided to show her. We thought you'd be pleased to see us,' she added naïvely.

'Of course, of course,' he replied with mock gallantry.

Bronwyn came straight to the point. 'How are the horses?'

He smiled. 'Quite well, thank you. I'll tell them you enquired.'

'Oh.' They looked at him in silent expectation until Bronwyn uttered a deep sigh, then said in a sorrowful voice, 'We've been told they're all booked for this afternoon, and we've come in our jeans—*specially.*'

'Specially to ride along the beach?' He raised one brow in her direction. 'Well, as it happens they *were* all booked until a short time ago, but now two people have changed their minds about riding and will be going for a bush walk instead.'

'So?' they breathed together, their brown eyes wide with hope.

'So I guess the horses you rode last time will be available.'

'*Oh, thank you!*' Their gratitude was accompanied by triumphant glances thrown at Lana, and then Raewyn's voice became raised with excitement. 'You'll see that we've remembered all you told us about knees and heels and hands and elbows.'

Lana sent a rueful smile towards Eunice. 'Wouldn't you know that those two would get their way?'

But Eunice hardly heard her. Speaking anxiously to Brent, she said, 'You'll be riding with the girls?'

Brent shook his head. 'No. I'm taking guests for a bush walk. But don't worry about the girls, Mrs Glenny, the stableman will be keeping an eye on this afternoon's riding party.'

The twins looked crestfallen but realised they would be unable to persuade Brent to change his plans, so they made an effort to exchange a few pleasantries with Camille.

But Camille hardly heard them. She had had little to say and she now spoke to Brent in a voice that was almost pleading. 'Would there be room for me in the station wagon? I'd like to come to the bush if you'll take me.'

He made no attempt to hide his surprise. 'Yes, there's one seat left, but I thought you disliked bush walks.'

'Oh, no, you're mistaken,' she declared hastily, then added with a show of enthusiasm, 'I'm most interested in all the activities arranged by Leisure Lodge. But you know that, Brent.' Her eyes glittered like green lights as she gazed at him, then she turned to send a challenging glare towards Lana.

The action was not lost upon Eunice, who asked with interest, 'Do you live here permanently, Mrs Boyd?'

'No, not yet.' Then defiantly, 'But the time might come when I shall. If you must know, I've been considering applying for a job here,' she added with what sounded like a degree of confidence.

The statement was met by silence from the people at both tables until Brent gave a short laugh. 'You've got to be joking,' he said. 'I can't see you as a housemaid, or working in the kitchen.'

'Neither of those situations had crossed my mind,' Camille replied with a show of dignity. 'Actually I was thinking of the desk job. Lana won't be there for much longer.'

Brent's brow darkened. 'The desk? What do you mean? Aren't you forgetting that Peggy will be returning?'

She sent him an arch look. 'Haven't you heard the news?'

'News? What news? What are you talking about?'

Camille leaned towards him in a confidential manner. 'Hilary told me that Peggy won't be coming back. A letter from her came this morning, and that's when I got this idea.'

Brent turned to Eric. 'Is this true?'

He nodded gloomily. 'I'm afraid it is. Even Lana has only just learned of the situation.' He sent her an apologetic grin. 'You'll recall that the mail was late this morning, and by the time I'd come to Peggy's letter you were involved with your mother and sisters.'

Camille said, 'When Hilary told me that Peg wouldn't be coming back I knew at once that I'd like the desk job.'

Brent interrupted impatiently. 'Is it possible for me to be told exactly why Peggy isn't coming back?'

Eric said, 'Apparently her mother suffered a slight stroke

a few days after the wedding, and now, with her sister married and away from home, Peggy realises she can't leave her mother, especially for a job that's so far away. So, when Lana leaves we'll have to advertise for a receptionist,' he added, despite Camille's former remarks about stepping into the position.

Raewyn directed a sly look towards Brent. 'Daddy is wondering when Lana will be back in the office. He's missing her.'

'Then she can go at once and I'll take over,' Camille suggested eagerly. 'I'm sure Hilary and I will get on famously in—in running the place.' She smiled happily, giving the impression she considered the question to be settled.

'Can you type?' Eric snapped at her.

Camille was startled. 'No, but I'll learn.'

'I don't intend to wait for a new receptionist to learn typing,' he gritted, making no attempt to conceal his irritation. 'In any case, the matter will be discussed in private between Brent, Hilary and myself, and in the meantime the arrangement made with Lana has not yet run its course.'

Camille smiled, first at Eric and then at Brent. 'I can wait,' she said, again with confidence. 'I'll be ready when you are.' Her eyes slid to Lana, this time holding a gleam of triumph.

The last few minutes of conversation had left Lana feeling dazed. Peggy would not be returning, and when she herself left the desk would be taken over by Camille, at least if things went the redhead's way. It would place her closer to Brent, and within a short time he might even begin to realise he did love her after all. Perhaps a deep affection for her was lying dormant. It could rise to the surface and—and——

Further thoughts became unbearable, sending something

in the nature of a sharp pain through her. It completely
ruined her appetite, and she found herself unable to eat the
food placed before her. And while she sat staring at the
salad on her plate, Raewyn's voice pierced her thoughts.

'Why don't you offer the position to Lana as a permanent
job?' she queried. 'I know she loves being here and it would
solve the problem.'

A snigger escaped Camille. 'That's most unlikely to
happen.'

Eunice turned to face her. 'Oh? Why not?' she asked
sharply. 'Are you suggesting that Lana has been
unsatisfactory? I understood she'd been quite the opposite.'

Camille sent her an enigmatic smile. 'There are more
ways than one of being—satisfactory, Mrs Glenny.'

'What do you mean?' Eunice persisted quietly.

Lana knew a moment of panic. 'Please leave it, Mother,'
she pleaded urgently, fearing the conversation was edging
towards dangerous ground, and knowing that Camille was
more than capable of hinting at a romantic alliance between
Eric and her. It would bring forth an angry reaction from
Eunice, possibly one that would reveal her true relationship
to him.

Brent came to her rescue. 'Lana's right. The subject must
be dropped, otherwise we'll have the twins applying for the
job,' he added teasingly by way of dispelling the tension
that was beginning to cloud the atmosphere.

'We can type,' Bronwyn told him proudly. 'Rae and I
have been going to commercial college, and at the end of
our course we begin as juniors in Daddy's firm, so when
Lana leaves to get married she'll hardly be missed at all.'

Her words were followed by a tense silence until Camille
turned to Lana and said sweetly, 'You didn't tell us you had
marriage in view. How very nice for you. I'm sure we all
hope you'll be happy.'

Lana opened her mouth to speak, then became aware of

Brent's narrowed gaze resting upon her, his eyes holding an icy glint.

His voice came smoothly. 'Indeed, this is a surprise. Why was it necessary for you to have been so secretive?'

She longed to shout that it was just a load of rubbish, that it was merely another sample of Bronwyn's stupid babbling. And then the expression on his face, the tightness about his mouth, caused the denial to die on her lips.

Obviously he was recalling the moments he had held her in his arms and her willing response to his kisses. His memories were causing him to stamp her as a two-timing flirt who was ready to fell into the arms of any man who came her way, and naturally this would include Eric. Very well, let him think as he wished.

'May we know the name of the lucky man?' Brent pursued.

Lana glared at him unflinchingly while endeavouring to keep her voice steady. 'Perhaps Mother could tell you.'

But Eunice merely shook her head in a bewildered fashion. 'I'm afraid this is news to me. I had no idea that Lana had such plans.'

Lana turned to Brent, her gaze still steadily cold. 'Then why not ask your informant?' she suggested. 'No doubt Bronwyn can give you a few more details, perhaps even the date and time of the wedding.'

Brent turned to the younger girl. 'OK, Bronwyn, what's the name of this fellow Lana is to marry?'

Bronwyn gulped, then flushed to find herself the centre of attention. She cast a nervous glance towards Raewyn as she admitted, 'Oh, there isn't anyone special at the *moment*. I didn't say she had definite plans *now*. I meant that *sooner or later* Lana would leave to get married, and when that time comes, if it ever does——'

Raewyn interrupted her twin's explanation. 'It was Mrs Boyd who jumped to the conclusion that Lana had plans to get married.'

Eric said, 'That's what I call a real anticlimax.' He stood up and put a kindly hand on Lana's shoulder. 'I'll relieve Hilary at the desk. There's no need for you to hurry back to it.'

'Thank you.' She smiled at him gratefully, at the same time being aware that Brent's eyes still watched her reaction to the older man.

Hilary entered the room a few minutes later, and as she sent a smile to everyone at the two tables she remarked pleasantly, 'This looks as if it's a family party.'

Camille spoke to her eagerly. Not being interested in anything that looked like a family party, she asked, 'Did Eric tell you I'm to be considered?'

A veiled expression crept into Hilary's eyes. 'Considered for what?'

'For the reception job, of course. Now that Peggy's not coming back I can start the moment Lana leaves.'

'That's interesting.' Hilary's tone was non-committal while her eyes sent questions towards Brent. 'I've never thought of you in a job of any sort. You lead such a life of leisure.'

'Then Leisure Lodge is the right place for me,' Camille quipped, then went on hastily, 'I know you'll be having a meeting about it, but of course Brent will have the final say.' Her green eyes shone with confidence as she turned to look at him.

'Naturally, he'll have the final say,' Hilary agreed in a dry tone as she picked up the menu and began to study it.

Camille sent Brent a dazzling smile. 'Do you know, I believe he's already come to a decision.'

Brent's face was inscrutable as he said quietly, 'My decision will rest upon what is best for the smooth running of the guest-house. The livelihood of the entire staff depends upon its success, and there's to be no dissension between the people in charge of operations.'

'Hilary and I have always been such good friends,' Camille

hastened to assure him.

'Really? I hadn't noticed.' Brent's tone was ironic, then he turned to Hilary as though waiting for confirmation of this statement.

But Hilary did not reply. Instead she gave her order to Betty who had approached the table.

Brent glanced at his watch, then stood up. 'If you'll excuse me I'll check that the horses have been brought into the yard. Be at the stables in half an hour,' he told the twins.

'We'll be there,' they echoed with unconcealed excitement.

He spoke to Camille. 'The bush walk will also leave in thirty minutes. Make sure you wear suitable shoes.'

'I will,' she promised eagerly. 'And I'll see that everyone else is wearing correct walking-shoes. It'll be the first of my duties in this place.'

Nobody answered this final remark and there was silence as they watched Brent leave this room, a tall figure striding between the tables, his progress also followed by the eyes of other guests.

Looking at the faces of the latter, Lana realised that the dining-room appeared to be filled with new people. It brought home the fact that Leisure Lodge was a place where guests came and went without being missed, although she had to admit that she was missing the incorrigible Claramae Crosby and her husband, who had now left to continue their travels in other parts of New Zealand.

But would she herself be missed when she returned to Wellington? She doubted it. And then the thought of Camille's taking her place at the desk filled her with a deep despair which she knew must be kept under control for the rest of the afternoon, otherwise it would be noticed by Eunice's sharp eyes.

However, this did not prove to be as difficult as she had expected because activities at the desk kept her occupied; furthermore, they helped to obliterate the sight of Camille sitting close to Brent as the station wagon drove away from the front steps.

In the meantime Eunice relaxed in a comfortable veranda chair, busily engaged with her tapestry needlework while awaiting the twins' return from their ride. They came at last, and as they prepared to leave Lana said with forced cheerfulness, 'I'll probably be home sooner than expected.'

Eunice said, 'Do you really think they'll give Mrs Boyd the job?'

Raewyn cut in before Lana could reply. 'We told the stableman she was angling for it.'

'And he nearly laughed his head off,' Bronwyn interrupted. 'He said if she got it, it would be over Hilary's dead body.'

But during the following days the memory of these words did little to comfort Lana, because Camille formed the habit of hovering near the desk, obviously watching and learning all she could about the job. There were occasions when she answered the phone, snatching the receiver before Lana could lay her hand on it, and there were times when she took it upon herself to usher new arrivals into their rooms.

She even reached the stage of discussing with Hilary which rooms should be allotted, and it also seemed clear that Hilary was well aware of Camille's endeavours. Her attitude towards them appeared to be one of amused tolerance, and to make matters worse her utter complacency made Lana wonder if she was actually encouraging Camille's activities. So much for the stableman's opinion, she thought bitterly as the situation became more and more frustrating.

At one stage her irritation almost caused her to rush into the office to tell Eric she would be leaving that evening, but even as she reached the door the sight of the two sailing-vessels on the wall caused her to pause and realise there was still a little more information she would like to glean from him.

The opportunity came with the next batch of letters to be typed, and as she went into the office to do them Camille settled herself at the desk. 'Don't bother to hurry,' she assured Lana airily. 'I can manage quite well and soon I'll be here all the time.'

Lana ignored the remark, then went into the office to find herself alone with Eric. She worked rapidly, although at times her eyes strayed towards the oil paintings, and at last she left her seat to stand below the *Hovding*. Gazing at its three tall masts, its taut rigging and its canvas billowing as it rode the white-crested waves, she said, 'Tell me, Eric, what caused your forebears to come to New Zealand?' It was a question she had meant to ask on several occasions because they were also her own forebears.

'Promises brought them here,' he told her. 'Promises of opportunity and a better life. At the time conditions in their own country were bad and there seemed to be little or no prospect of improvement.'

'The promises must have been good to persuade them to leave homes and loved ones to sail to the other side of the world,' she said thoughtfully. 'Who made these promises?'

'The New Zealand Government of the day. They needed men who could construct roads and railways through large tracts of dense bush, so they looked to the Scandinavian countries where they'd find hardworking people who were used to chilly weather and lumber work.'

'I see. And so they came. The months at sea must have been a nightmare, full of dangers and hardships.'

'But nothing to the hardships they found when they reached their destination.' He told her about some of the ordeals faced by those people, then added, 'The land of milk and honey they'd been promised was at the end of some other rainbow.'

'The mere thought of facing storms in a sailing-ship is enough to make me shudder,' Lana confessed.

He came to stand beside her. 'The *Hovding* was known as a clipper. She was sharp-bowed and built for speed, and she made the voyage in one hundred and eight days.' He paused, then placed one hand on her shoulder in a friendly gesture that caused them to stand closer to each other. Then with the other hand he pointed out various aspects of the ship's canvas. 'All the sails have names,' he told her. 'That's the main topgallant, and that's the mizzen topgallant. Those angled sails stretching beyond the bow are known as jibs. That's the flying jib, the outer jib, the inner jib.'

His head had come closer to hers, but she made no move to draw away until she was startled by the sound of Hilary's voice coming from the doorway.

'Are you thinking of sailing away with her, Eric?' she asked, her voice shaking from an emotion she found difficult to control.

They turned, to face not only Hilary but also Brent who stood beside her. Lana noticed the hardness in his face, the grim lines about his mouth, and she quailed beneath the accusation in his eyes. Beyond Brent and Hilary stood Camille, a broad smile on her face.

Hilary's lip curled as she said, 'If it hadn't been for Camille we'd have missed this touching scene. Brent and I were talking on the veranda when she called us in to take a peep in the office.'

'May I ask what you expected them to see?' Eric gritted at Camille.

'I wasn't sure how far you'd have progressed,' she admitted smugly.

'What the hell do you mean by progressed?' he lashed at her.

'Well, I was sitting at the desk when I realised I couldn't

hear the typewriter,' Camille told him. 'Work seemed to have come to a stop, so I peeped in to see what was happening. You appeared to be standing very close together, and I felt you'd have her in your arms at any moment. And if that happened I knew it was something that Hilary—and Brent—should see for themselves.'

Eric gave a loud snort of derision before he said scathingly, 'Do you honestly believe I'd be kissing Lana with you only yards away? You must be less intelligent than I imagined, Camille.' He paused, then glared coldly at Hilary. 'And apparently that mental state applies to you too, my dear.'

Lana said quickly, her tone stinging, 'There's no need to ask what Brent thinks. He hasn't said a word, but it's written all over his face.'

This was indeed a fact. Brent had come further into the room, his watchful eyes moving from Lana to Eric, his expression one of accusation, while a muscle pulsing beside his hard jaw indicated his barely controlled anger.

Lana looked at the tightness of his well-shaped mouth, then turned to Eric as she said frankly, 'I suppose you do realise he suspects us of having an affair? He's positive I'm drawn towards men much older than myself.'

Eric looked nonplussed. 'No, I hadn't realised, and what's more I thought my wife trusted me. However, I can understand Brent's being jealous.'

'He's not jealous,' Lana said with a bitterness she was unable to disguise. 'He couldn't care two hoots on a tin whistle about *me*. He's completely wrapped up with the smooth running of the guest-house.' She swung round to face Brent. 'Isn't that so, oh master of Leisure Lodge?'

He had seated himself on the edge of a table, his arms folded across his chest as he continued to watch the people in the room. 'It might surprise you to learn that my emotions are not entirely dominated by the guest-house,' he retorted crisply.

'No? You could have fooled me,' Lana snapped back.

He left the table and moved closer to look down into her face. 'Your memory of certain moments is so short?' he asked quietly.

She knew he meant the memory of his kisses, the times he had held her against him, and the deep longing they had felt for each other when on the riverbank. 'I remember things that are true and sincere, things that are *meant*,' she said, hoping he would get the message.

He frowned, still staring down into her face. 'What makes you so sure they were insincere?'

The question gave her the crazy feeling they were the only two people in the room. However, she knew that this was not so, so she answered carefully. 'What was there to tell me they were meant—that they were not merely a passing whim?'

'I'm surprised by your lack of judgement.'

'Sorry, I'm not clairvoyant.'

Hilary interrupted crossly, 'What are you two going on about?'

Lana ignored her as she continued to gaze up into Brent's face. Recently she had realised that her days at Leisure Lodge were numbered, and suddenly she knew that the last number had come up. It was time for her to leave, and the words left her lips unwillingly as she said, 'You'll be pleased to know that any problems you've had concerning me are over. I'm going to my room to pack. I'm leaving at once.'

The statement brought an exclamation of displeasure from Eric. 'Hey, wait a minute, you can't go yet! You haven't finished these letters,' he protested.

'Let Camille try to do them,' Lana suggested. 'And what's more, she's welcome to the desk job. I'll be glad to get away from the atmosphere of suspicion that's hung over my head from the moment I agreed to take Peggy's place.' She felt so frustrated and angry she hardly knew what she was saying, and she also knew that tears were not far away.

'You can't leave today,' Brent said with determination.

His words surprised Lana. 'Indeed? Who's to stop me?'

'I'm stopping you, because I'm taking you to the island tomorrow. I've already arranged with the chef to prepare a hamper of food.'

She was so taken aback that for several moments she could only stare at him in silence. But at last she gathered her wits and managed to say, 'Thank you, I no longer have any wish to go there.'

'Why not? You were keen enough the last time I mentioned it.'

'Things have changed since then. That was when I thought you might believe there was nothing of a romantic nature between Eric and me. But now I can see I was mistaken in harbouring that hope, the sooner I go home the better it will be for everyone, and of course for the smooth running of the lodge,' she flung at him.

Hilary made an effort to take command of the situation. She moved to Lana's side and said earnestly, 'I think you're making a mistake in not going to the island with Brent. It's a lovely day's outing. Personally I consider you'd be wise to avail yourself of the opportunity, because it's not everyone who can get across to Kapiti.'

Hilary's words surprised Lana. Was it possible that the older woman approved of her spending a whole day alone in Brent's company? Could it be that she was encouraging them to be together? But before she could decide upon replies to either of these questions Hilary spoke again, this time her words being accompanied by a smile.

'Why don't we all forget this quarrelsome scene?' she asked with forced cheerfulness. 'Lana, why don't you finish those letters for Eric, and then we'll go on as though it had never happened, and tomorrow Brent will give you a marvellous day out in the launch.'

'A very good idea,' Camille exclaimed. 'I'll go with them.'

'Like hell you will!' Brent snarled at her. 'You say you want the desk job. Very well, you can prove yourself worthy of it by attending to it tomorrow.'

Camille pouted. 'I don't want to be at the desk tomorrow. I'm coming to Kapiti with you. I'm still a guest, and your brochure advertises horse-riding, bush walks and launch trips for guests.'

'This is not a guest trip,' he cut in. 'This is a staff trip in the form of a bonus, and you're not yet on the staff.'

'You're splitting hairs,' Camille argued.

'So what? The point is that I promised Lana a trip to Kapiti and I don't want it ruined by snide remarks.'

'Snide remarks? I like that!' Camille was indignant.

'Your attitude towards her has been obvious to most people,' he pointed out calmly.

Camille shrugged. 'Oh, well, if you're only keeping a promise.'

The remark hit Lana with force. Of course that was all it was. His ego demanded that he must keep his word. He must do what he had said he would do. Her chin rose as she turned to face him. 'Camille is right. You're merely satisfying your own self-esteem by keeping a promise, so in that case you can forget it. I shan't go to Kapiti with you. And now I'll pack my bags.'

But her move towards the door was waylaid by Hilary's grip on her arm. 'Please don't do that,' the older woman pleaded. 'At least finish the letters first.'

'Let her go,' Eric said gruffly. 'I'll manage somehow, although I would never have believed Lana would leave me in the lurch.'

A wild laugh escaped Lana. 'My goodness, that's really funny!'

'What's funny?' grumbled Eric. 'I see nothing humorous in this situation.'

'It's just the thought that *I* should be the one who's leaving *you* in the lurch,' she exclaimed, then stopped abruptly, shocked by the sound of the careless words tumbling from her lips. She was relieved to find they had little impact on the others, because they merely looked at her blankly, unable to understand what had amused her.

Brent was the first to break the silence following her outburst. 'Can you honestly say you have no wish to come to Kapiti tomorrow?' he asked in a low voice.

Her eyes held a bleak expression. 'No, I can't honestly say that.'

'Then you will come? You'll promise not to disappear in the night?'

She nodded. 'Yes, I'll come.' Of course she wanted to go with him. Loving him as she did, she longed to be at his side, and tomorrow would be the last opportunity to enjoy such a luxury. It had been her silly pride that had made her say she wouldn't go. The thought that he was taking her for the sake of keeping a promise had got under her skin.

Then Eric sat down before the typewriter. He rolled a letter-head paper into the machine and began stabbing at the keys with two fingers. 'What's the date?' he enquired, a pained expression on his face.

It was too much for Lana. 'I'll do it,' she offered, resigned.

Eric's gloom lifted as he stood up with alacrity. 'I'd be most grateful, thank you.'

Lana tried to ignore the others as she made an effort to concentrate on the work before her. She sensed that Brent was regarding her intently and she tried to refrain from looking up to meet his gaze, so it was a relief when he sat at his table and drew a calculator and a pile of accounts towards him.

She also knew that Eric had sat down again and was now shuffling through papers on his table. A quick peep showed angry lines about his mouth and she guessed he was still annoyed with Hilary for doubting him, and possibly with Camille for having caused the scene.

Hilary spoke to Camille, her voice cool with suppressed irritation. 'I think it's time we had a talk, Camille. Shall we leave the others to get on with their work?'

Camille gave a short laugh. 'Do you mean we should leave them to get on with the smooth running of the place?' she asked, giving undue emphasis to the last words.

'Yes, as it happens that's exactly what I want to talk about. Shall we go somewhere private?'

Camille was momentarily nonplussed, then appeared to be flattered. A smile spread over her face as she said, 'You mean you want to discuss the smooth running with *me*? But there's no need to go into a corner to do that. Brent and Eric will want to hear our decisions. As for Lana, hasn't she already told you she'll be leaving?'

Hilary sounded exasperated. 'You're taking me up the wrong way, Camille. You don't appear to be getting my meaning.'

Camille stared at her.d 'Aren't we to discuss——?'

'The smooth running that you've been doing your utmost to disrupt,' Hilary snapped. 'The trouble you've caused this morning is only one example of it. And you're right, Eric and Brent should hear what I have to say on the matter. They'll be interested to learn you've been upsetting the guests.'

Camille's jaw sagged. 'Upsetting the guests? That's nonsense.' She sent an accusing glare towards Lana. 'Is this something she's been saying?'

'Certainly not,' retorted Hilary crisply. 'I happen to know it was because of you that the Crosbys left earlier than they had intended. When they were paying their account Mrs Crosby told me that you'd spoken rudely to her in the lounge and before other guests. Her husband was so annoyed he told her to pack at once.'

'I gave the woman what she deserved.' Camille defended herself hotly.

'Was there an argument?' Brent asked in mild tones.

'Well, yes, there was,' Camille admitted.

'Then suppose you tell us your side of it,' he said.

She beamed at him. 'Thank you, Brent, then perhaps I'll get a fair hearing, and it might also interest you to learn I was arguing on your behalf.' Her cheeks had become flushed as she uttered the last words.

His brows rose. 'Indeed? Tell me more.'

'That Crosby woman was telling a new arrival about the church at Otaki, and then she started discussing your private affairs.'

He frowned. 'What could she know about my private affairs?'

'I mean your *romantic* affair, if you could call it that.'

'I'm afraid I'm still in the dark,' he said.

Camille's hesitation was only momentary, then her words came with a rush. 'That woman told everyone in the lounge that it had been just lovely to see you standing before the altar with—with *her*.' She paused to glare balefully at Lana. 'So I let her have it right from the shoulder. I told her there was little fear of Lana marrying you because she was completely taken up with Eric. The silly woman began to rant and rave about it being a pack of lies, but you and Hilary know it's true, even if Eric is too blind to see it for himself.' She paused to draw breath.

Lana felt herself go hot and then cold, and although she longed to scream and shout the truth her instinct told her that somebody else would handle the matter of this particular situation, and this proved to be correct when Brent appeared to take control.

'Have you quite finished?' he asked, his voice dangerously quiet.

'I suppose so.' Camille's expression had become sulky, perhaps because her explanation had not brought forth the sympathetic hearing she had expected. 'But you do see that I was arguing on your behalf?' she persisted anxiously.

Brent's tone became dry. 'Thank you, Camille. I assure you it was quite unnecessary, and in future I'd prefer that you did not argue on my behalf.' He turned to Hilary, and giving her the cue for her next move he asked, 'Aren't we expecting a coachload of senior citizens tomorrow?'

'Yes, they'll be here by late afternoon.'

'The accommodation for these elderly people is satisfactory?' Brent pursued. 'As manageress of this place you've made sure it's not too cramped?' His words seemed to be loaded with meaning.

Hilary betrayed a moment of startled surprise as she caught the message. 'Well, actually the accommodation is somewhat tight.' She faced Camille squarely and said, 'I'm afraid we'll be needing your room, Camille. If you'll vacate it in the morning it can be serviced before the coach arrives.'

Camille drew a sharp breath, then went crimson with anger. 'Are you asking me to leave? Am I being put out?'

'I didn't intend to put it quite so bluntly,' Hilary replied calmly. 'However, you know your stay with us has been much longer than usual and without a date of termination. When the coach reservations were made I didn't realise you'd still be here.'

Camille interrupted her. 'Brent knows why I'm here.' She looked at him pleadingly. 'You know why I've stayed so long, don't you, Brent?'

His face was unsmiling. 'I presumed it was for the same reasons that other people stay here, for sea, sun and sand. You've always declared it saves you from setting up your own beach house.'

'That's right,' Eric put in. 'I've heard you say so on several occasions.'

'You've said it over and over again,' Hilary echoed.

Camille ignored their comments as she said to Brent, 'You know it was for more than that.'

He regarded her coolly. 'Do I? I can't imagine what more

there could be around these parts,' he drawled. 'At least, apart from the odd bush walk, a few horseback rides or fishing-trips.'

She became desperate. 'Brent, you *know* I'm not here for those things, you *know* it's for more than that. What about out—our deep *friendship*?'

'I trust we'll always be friends, Camille,' he informed her gravely, his voice almost compassionate.

Hilary came to Brent's rescue, her voice taking on a businesslike briskness as she said to Camille, 'I'm sure you know that ten o'clock is the usual time for vacating a room. I'll go and make up your account.'

She left the office and Camille had little option but to follow her. Their departure left a silence, and from the corner of her eye Lana watched Brent continue with his accounts. His face was a mask, and she wondered if his mind was really on the figures being tapped on the calculator.

He had been diplomatic, she decided. He had not hurt Camille by denying their friendship, nor had he upset Hilary by removing the management of the situation from her capable hands. Smiling inwardly, Lana had to admit to herself that he was indeed lord of the lodge.

CHAPTER TEN

WHEN Lana woke next morning she felt strangely calm, as though a load had been removed from her shoulders. Lying in bed, she thought about it, wondering what had wrapped her in such peaceful tranquillity, until she realised it stemmed from the knowledge that Camille would be leaving that day.

There was also the fact that Hilary's distrust concerning her and Eric appeared to have evaporated, but this did not mean that all suspicion concerning this point had been removed from Brent's mind. This was an entirely different matter, and she feared that only time would convince him there had been nothing erotic between her and his manager. And by that time he would have forgotten her. She would be just another of the many people who had come to the lodge and who had later gone their way. Already Peggy was becoming somebody from the past.

She recalled the scene of the previous afternoon when Hilary had actually asked Camille to leave. It had been done with the utmost dignity and without too much unpleasantness, the pending arrival of the senior citizens giving Hilary as manageress the necessary excuse for needing Camille's room.

Recollection of the tour coach's arrival filled Lana with dismay, causing her to realise that this was not a day to be going to Kapiti Island. It was a day when she should be at the desk, ready to help in showing people their rooms, or to give any necessary information. However, it was possible that Brent had already thought of this and had decided to postpone the trip.

She sprang out of bed and looked at the jeans and protective blue jersey she had intended wearing, then regretfully laid them aside, feeling sure that the trip would be put off. And this seemed to be even more likely when she went in for breakfast and was greeted by a cold glare from Camille.

The redhead's lip curled into a sneer as her eyes ran over Lana's usual office attire. 'Not dressed for the launch? Am I to understand that your day out with Brent has been put off?' She gave an exaggerated sigh. 'Oh dear, how sad! Of course, if my stay had not been curtailed Hilary would have had my help at the desk when all those old dears arrive. But now your day has been ruined. Too bad!' The words ended with a short laugh.

Lana forced herself to smile sweetly. 'There'll be another day,' was all she said, then she concentrated on her breakfast. A short time later she made her way to relieve Hilary at the desk, and while there she saw Camille carry her bags out to her car, then drive away without a word of farewell to anyone.

Hilary did not remain long at her breakfast, and when she returned to the desk she looked at Lana's dress with a hint of surprise. 'Are you ready for your day's outing with Brent?'

'Are we really going?' The question came doubtfully.

'If you go out to the veranda you'll see the launch. Brent has already put a hamper of food on board.'

'But I thought you'd need me here. I mean, with this coach tour arriving——'

Brent came out of the office and spoke from behind her. 'Don't worry about the senior citizens, they're not due before late afternoon. We'll be home before they arrive.'

Hilary spoke earnestly to Lana, her voice betraying anxiety. 'Will you make sure about that? Will you please help him to keep an eye on the time? He's inclined to forget any other place exists when he's over there.'

'I'll do my best,' Lana promised, feeling doubtful that she could order Brent to head for home, and knowing it was the last thing that she herself would be wanting to do. Excitement began to mount within her, causing her eyes to sparkle and a flush to tinge her cheeks.

Looking at him she realised he was definitely dressed for the launch trip. The red and black check shirt covering his broad shoulders was open at the neck, revealing the crisp dark hairs on his chest. The grey shorts encasing his slim hips left his long muscled legs bare, and it was only with an effort that she kept her eyes from them. She was reminded of the first time she had met him. It had been on her first day here when she had wondered if a Greek god had stepped from the water.

'There's another point to remember,' said Hilary, cutting into Lana's musings. 'When a coachload arrives Eric and I like Brent to be at the door to welcome people in the manner of a true host. Not odd arrivals, you understand, but a coachload is different.'

Eric spoke from the office doorway, his tone joking as he said, 'We've tried to persuade him to wear a white apron and to bow low from the waist in the manner of the old-time host, but he draws the line at that caper.'

Brent laughed as he said to Lana, 'Now you can see why they're kept on to run the place. They add such finesse to the job. You can stop worrying, Hilary, we'll be home in good time.'

'All right, but don't forget that the coach arrives at five o'clock, so that means you should be home by four-thirty at the latest.' Her voice still held its anxious note.

'OK, OK, we'll be home long before then,' he asured her, then turning to regard Lana his eyes inspected her attire. 'I expected to find you dressed in jeans and a jersey. There'll be a cool breeze out there.'

'I thought the trip would be put off,' she explained.

'Certainly not. Go and change at once, and smother your face with plenty of suntan lotion. Bring the bottle with you.'

Lana needed no further bidding. She hurried to her bedroom, and as she changed into her jeans she almost toppled over from sheer excitement. She flung her blue jersey over her head, and her hands trembled as she rubbed suntan lotion into her face and neck, then snatching up her hat she returned to the office.

Brent surveyed her critically. 'That's better, although your hat will have to be tied securely.' He placed it on her head and made a double bow of the ribbons beneath her chin.

'He thinks you need a nanny,' Eric chuckled.

Brent ignored the remark while Lana glowed inwardly from the knowledge that he was really taking care of her. She almost skipped with joy as they made their way across the lawn towards the track leading down to the beach, and as they reached it Hilary's voice made them pause to look back. 'Don't forget the coach is due at five!' she shouted from the veranda.

Brent merely waved to her and they went down to where the launch's dinghy rested near the edge of the ripples. They pushed it out together and were soon at the vessel's side. 'Welcome aboard the *Leisure*,' he said.

Minutes later the anchor was up and they were heading towards the southern end of Kapiti's six-mile length. Exhilaration filled Lana as she stood beside Brent whose hand rested lightly on the wheel, and although the sea's slight choppiness sent spray over the bow they were sheltered from it by the cabin.

As they drew near to the island the long hump lost its misty blue tinge, its wooded hills and valleys becomng massed by myriad shades of green. The three small islets and groups of rocks also became clearer, and as they approached she listened to Brent's deep voice pointing out various landmarks while telling her of the large Maori population and the whaling stations that once existed on the island.

'Does anyone live on Kapiti now?' she asked, finding difficulty in visualising those distant days.

'Only the caretaker. I've already been in touch with him to get permission to land. He's known as the ranger.'

She turned to look at his handsome profile. 'You seem to think of everything. I suspect that you always do the right thing.'

'I don't like to have that sort of reputation,' he admitted gloomily. 'People never make allowances for the fact that I, also, can make mistakes.'

She laughed. 'It takes a big man to admit he's wrong, especially where a woman is concerned.'

He made no reply as he stared across the bow, nor did she wish to interrupt his train of thought. However, when he did decide to break the silence it was to change the subject. 'Kapiti is a strange island,' he told her. 'It covers five thousand acres, yet is only one and a half miles in width. Before we land I'll show you the western side which is merely a line of bare high cliffs, some rising to a thousand feet. Of course the place is full of legends.'

As they sailed clear of the rocks at the island's southern point memory swept Lana back to when they had stood at the window in the honeymoon suite. It was there he had said he liked to think of newly married couples gazing beyond the south end, and then his arms had gone about her. The recollection caused her to draw a deep breath.

He looked at her sharply. 'You're all right? Not seasick?'

'No, thank goodness. I was just looking at those two rocks.'

He followed her gaze. 'Those two on the island? They're the two dogs. Legend has it that in the dim past they belonged to a Maori woman from the South Island. Her husband abandoned her on Kapiti, so she walked into the water and swam home, a mere trifle of thirty miles. Her two dogs were afraid to follow her, so they went back to the cliff and sat waiting for her to return until eventually they became petrified.'

'Faithful hounds,' she murmured. 'More faithful than the husband.' She fell silent as she became conscious of his eyes resting upon her, one brow slightly raised in an unspoken question. Was he thinking of her association with Eric? At the moment she had no wish for this subject to be discussed, so she veered away from it by saying, 'Isn't the water rather rough on this side?'

'Yes, we'll return to leeward.' He spun the wheel and within a short time they were gliding in the calm waters that edged the eastern shore.

She watched anxiously when rocks seemed to be close, but eventually a small bay came into view. Brent steered the launch towards it, and after dropping the anchor he helped her into the dinghy. The hamper and a rug were also placed in the dinghy, and as he rowed the short distance to the shore he said, 'We'll have lunch in the bush.'

When they stepped from the dinghy Lana carried the rug while Brent lifted the hamper ashore. He led her towards an opening in the trees that grew down to a low level, but before entering it she turned to gaze across the water at the mainland, and at the lengthy line of mountain ranges stretching along the lower North Island. It all seemed to be so far away.

He came to stand beside her. 'Is something worrying you?'

'No, of course not. It's—it's just the isolation. There's a remoteness about this place.'

'The mainland is little more than four miles away, but if you're afraid of being alone with me we can always visit the ranger. I'm sure he'll help you keep me at bay.'

Her eyes became filled with reproach. 'Are you warning

me you're not to be trusted, or are you enjoying your little joke, your bout of mockery?' she asked accusingly.

His eyes glowered as they rested upon her. 'You might be interested to learn it's because of the way you affect me. One minute I long to give you a bear-hug, but the next instant I could shake hell out of you. I'm not accustomed to this type of frustration.'

His words came as a shock, causing her eyes to widen while she searched for words. They came at last when she said, '*I* frustrate *you*? I can hardly believe it.'

'Then you'd better believe it. Nor is there any need to go into details, because I'm sure you must be well aware of them.' His tone had developed an underlying grimness.

Eric, Lana thought bitterly, and again she shied away from discussing a topic that could only ruin her day.

Perhaps Brent also sensed the danger of a ruined day, because he turned abruptly and, carrying the hamper before him, pushed his way along a little-used track winding between the tree trunks. The ground was uneven, and thick undergrowth shut out the sight of the sea, but within a short time they came to a small flat area where he spread the rug and placed the hamper upon it. Then as he straightened his back he said, 'We'll take a short walk before we have lunch. I doubt that you'll need your hat beneath the trees.'

She pulled at the ribbons beneath her chin, but the double bow he had previously tied became knotted and refused to run free. He came closer to help, and as his fingers worked on the knot she could only stand and gaze up at his face. His expression remained serious, and as the ribbon became unravelled he surprised her by brushing his lips across hers before turning to walk along the path.

The unexected action made her pulses leap, but she was unable to dwell upon it because the vague track needed her full attention. It was not easy to follow as it had become overgrown by native grasses, and there was an eerie dimness

caused by numerous overhead branches which prevented
the sun from filtering through the thick foliage.

She said, 'I feel as though I'm walking in a magic land.
I've never had fantails fluttering so close to my head and
shoulders, yet I can't catch one.'

He chuckled. 'They're not really interested in us, but
they like the tiny insects we disturb as we walk.'

He stopped suddenly and drew her against him. Her
heart leapt and she expected to be kissed again, but he
merely pointed to a branch a short distance ahead. 'Can you
see them? They're wood pigeons.'

She gazed up at the plump birds, and as they stood
perfectly still a fantail's wing almost brushed her cheek
while her head rested against his shoulder.

They continued until the barely discernible track came to
an abrupt end, completely disappearing into a wilderness of
scrubby undergrowth, and as he frowned at what lay ahead
Brent said, 'I'm afraid we'll need to go back. In any case I
keep thinking of that hamper of food. It's time we had
lunch.'

As they retraced their steps a chorus of musical notes
echoed above their heads, forcing them to pause and listen
to the ringing of bell-like chimes. 'Tuis,' said Brent.
'They're black with white tufts at their throats.' His arm
went about her shoulder again as he drew her nearer to him
while they peered up into the branches, vainly searching for
the feathered songsters. 'They're too high to be seen,' he
said, then removed his arm and continued ahead of her
until they reached the place where the rug and hamper had
been left.

These are magic moments, thought Lana, sitting on the
rug and watching him open the hamper, and then an
exclamation of surprise escaped her as he extracted a bottle
of white wine and two stemmed glasses. 'Wine, at a picnic!'
She peered into the hamper. 'The chef has thought of

everything. There's a cold chicken, punnets of coleslaw and potato salad, hard-boiled eggs, tomatoes and crusty buttered rolls——'

'He probably guessed it was our first picnic, so it called for a special hamper,' he said gravely, handing her a filled goblet.

She looked at him wonderingly. 'Our first? You sound as though it might not be the last.'

'Anything's possible,' he returned non-committally.

She stared down at the pale sparkling liquid. 'Well, thank you for this one. I'm grateful to have been given the opportunity to set foot on Kapiti. It's a fascinating place.'

'It's a place where birds can live without fear of predators, and its history has always interested me,' he admitted, watching her serve food on to the picnic plates.

As they ate he recounted tales of the days when the island was a stronghold for the old Maori chief, and when the shores across the water echoed to the bloodthirsty yells of tribal warfare.

Lana sipped her wine and listened with interest, and while she revelled in the sound of his voice she wished they could remain in this Eden for countless hours. However, the leisurely meal came to an end, and as an occupation to keep her eyes from his face she began to replace all they had used into the hamper.

He removed it from where it rested on the rug between them then said, 'The wine isn't finished. Pass your glass.'

'You finish it,' she pleaded. 'I'm already feeling a little light-headed. More wine is sure to make me giggly and too talkative. I could become worse than the twins.'

'That might not be a bad idea,' he remarked, filling her glass despite her protest. 'I'd like to get you into a state of being too talkative. I'm sure it would be interesting.'

'You are? I wonder why.' His words had surprised her.

'It's because I believe you've been holding out on me. I

think there are things I should know, so drink up and tell me all about it.' His voice held a serious note.

Her eyes sparkled at him from across the goblet. 'What would you like to know?' she asked, at the same time warning herself to guard her tongue.

'Well, question number one, why did you offer to step into the desk job? Was it because of Eric? I recall he wondered if he'd met you at some previous date.'

'Yes, he did have something to do with it.' Despite her resolution of a moment ago the admission slipped out between sips of wine.

'Ah, then the twins were correct when they said you preferred older men.' His voice had hardened.

'No, they were quite wrong. Actually they were lying.'

'Why would they invent that sort of tale?'

'The twins have their own mysterious reasons for most of their actions,' she prevaricated, taking a further sip from the goblet.

'But I can see you're drawn towards Eric,' Brent persisted. 'Why don't you come clean and admit it?'

His voice now held an even more intensive harshness and his eyes seemed to bore into hers, causing her to scramble within her mind for an answer. And then the draining of the goblet loosened her tongue sufficiently to cause her to say, 'Why do you want to know these things? You know I'll be leaving soon, so why should it matter whether or not I'm drawn to Eric? OK, I'll admit I *have* been drawn towards him, but as I told you before, it's not in the way you think. And please don't start up about the smooth running of the place, because the moment I've left I'll be forgotten. Like everyone else I'll be less than a memory. What I can't understand is why you should be worrying so unnecessarily.' Her voice had risen and she paused to draw breath. 'There now, I said the wine would make me too talkative.'

He looked at her in silence for several long moments

before he took the glass from her hand and put it in the hamper. 'You really don't understand?'

She shook her head. 'No, it's beyond me.'

'Then I'd better explain.' He edged closer, moving into a position which enabled him to take her in his arms. 'Can't you see that I love you? That's why I want answers to these questions, it's why I must have them.' His voice was now low and filled with emotion.

For a moment Lana wondered if too much wine had caused her to hear incorrectly. 'What did you say?' she asked uncertainly.

Brent spoke huskily. 'I said I love you. Does it mean anything to you?' His eyes raked her face anxiously.

She could only look at him in a dazed manner, then she nodded as she whispered, 'Yes, *oh, yes,* it means everything to me.'

'You really mean that? You're quite certain?'

Again she nodded. 'I've never been more certain of anything in my life.'

'Then tell me, my darling, tell me you love me.'

'I love you, Brent—I love you so much it hurts.' The words tumbled tremulously.

His enfolding arms held her more closely, pressing her back against the rug as his hard mouth came down to part the sweetness of her soft lips, and then he changed his position to lie beside her.

Her heart thudded, causing her pulses to race as her arms crept about his neck, and for several long minutes they lay as though locked in harmony, floating heavenwards in the joyous revelation of their love for each other, until she murmured, 'I didn't know you loved me, I had no idea.'

He trailed his lips across her closed lids. 'Can't you understand why I held it back? It's been a torment, an inner fire that wouldn't be put out. I couldn't get rid of the flame. You see, I was so sure you felt something for Eric. There were times when I caught you looking at him with such a definite fondness in your eyes.'

She struggled into a sitting position and looked at him seriously. 'Darling, the time has come when I must tell you——'

'About you and Eric?' he cut in sharply.

'Yes.'

He was suddenly tense. 'I've always known there was something. OK, go on, I can take it.' He lay back on the rug and closed his eyes while his jaw hardened.

'You look as though you're waiting to learn the worst.'

'I suppose you were infatuated with him when you first met. Well, I can understand infatuation.'

Lana laughed as she bent over him to kiss his cheek. 'Not even that. Do I have to repeat it's not what you imagine? Believe it or not, Eric Halversen is my father.'

His eyes flew open as he sat up abruptly. *Good grief!*'

She went on, 'I was the baby whose birth caused Ingrid's death. At that time he wouldn't even look at me, and he put me out for adoption. But when I grew up I found I wanted to look at *him*. I wanted to know about the type of man I'd sprung from.'

'You wanted to dig for your own roots.'

'That's right. Roots. But with every single one of them behind a closed door, it was most frustrating.'

He regarded her with interest. 'So how did this present situation arise? How did you find him? I suppose the passing of the Adult Adoption Act enabled you to trace him with the help of the Social Welfare department.'

'No, I was more than fortunate in not having to trace him through any official channels.' She told him about John Glenny's cousin who had been working at the home when she had been born, and how, through Rita, the Glennys had learned where her father was living. 'From the moment I knew where to find him the temptation to look at him was too great to resist,' she concluded.

'Does Eric know who you are?' The question came sharply.

She shook her head. 'No, nor have I had any intention of telling him.' She went on to explain her early plan of just looking at Eric, and perhaps of talking to him a little, and how the desk job and the opportunity to know him better had then proved too much to resist.

Brent said, 'He'll have to be told, and he'll sure be rocked.

'Please believe me, I had no intention of causing an upset of any kind. I didn't realise that Eric might be drawn towards me. The thought that I might look like my mother never entered my head.'

'He probably thought Ingrid had returned.' He took her in his arms and kissed her tenderly. 'There's just one more question to be settled, my dearest. Will you marry me?'

Lana nodded, unable to speak.

'Please let it be as soon as possible.'

'Yes, oh yes. Perhaps a quiet wedding in the Otaki church.'

'I couldn't wish for anything more perfect.'

A disturbing thought crossed her mind. 'Do you think Hilary will be upset? I mean about me being Eric's daughter.'

'Of course not. I think you'll find she'll be more than relieved to discover the true situation, and then she'll adjust to it quite well. Also, her relief to learn I'm marrying you instead of Camille will probably cause her to welcome you with open arms.'

Lana was silent, wishing she could feel as confident as Brent concerning Hilary's attitude towards her, and turning troubled eyes towards him she said, 'I still can't help wondering if Hilary will resent my presence when she realises I'm Ingrid's daughter.'

Brent's mouth hardened as a frown darkened his brow. 'That situation will be easily remedied. If Hilary shows the slightest hint of antagonism towards you their employment will be terminated.'

'But that would be terrible! They're both so capable, and the smooth running——'

'My dear, nobody is indispensable, and nobody will be allowed to make you feel uncomfortable or cause you unhappiness, not even for the sake of Leisure Lodge.'

His words caused a glow of confidence to flow through her, and suddenly she felt that perhaps Hilary would accept her for the sake of her own relations with Eric.

Brent said, 'Tomorrow we'll drive to Wellington to buy a ring, and I'd like to meet John Glenny.'

Lana shook her head. 'Not tomorrow. Not until the coach has taken the senior citizens on their way. Hilary will need my help.'

He chuckled. 'Are you actually putting the lodge before an engagement ring?'

'Well, it's Hilary, really. I know she'll need me to be there.'

'Bless you!' He took her in his arms again and for a while the world stood still. But at last he looked at his watch and said with regret, 'If we're to be home by four-thirty we'll have to start moving now. We could be slowed down by a tidal rip between here and the mainland.' He sat up with a sudden exclamation. 'Hell's teeth, I'd forgotten the tide! The launch mught be up on the beach.'

They picked up the rug and hamper, then hurried along the track towards the opening to the beach. When they reached it they found that Brent's fears had proved to be correct, because the receding tide had left the launch high and dry on the sand. It lay on its side and was obviously too heavy to be pushed towards the water.

Lana threw an anxious glance towards him. 'What now?'

she asked.

He shrugged. 'We'll just have to wait for the tide to come in. I'm afraid the coach will arrive long before we can get across.'

'Hilary will be furious.'

'She'll be more than furious. She'll be worried sick and in a panic. They'll both imagine the worst has happened. They'll fear we've hit one of the rocks round the island, or that the launch has sunk, or perhaps we've been overturned by a freak wave. They'll never think that I could have been stupid enough to forget the tide. Not me, I'm the reliable one who never makes mistakes.'

'Perhaps you had other things on your mind,' she suggested with feigned innocence.

'You can say that again!' He dropped the hamper and snatched her to him, crushing her against his body.

The embrace left her breathless, then she gasped as an unexpected movement swept her feet from the ground and she found herself cradled in his arms. Long strides bore her back to the opening in the trees where he laid her gently on the soft forest floor, and as her arms went about him he stretched his length beside her.

'My precious darling,' he murmured huskily.

Wordlessly, she clung to him while his mouth found hers, a surge of desire shaking her as his fingers fondled her taut nipples. His lips found their way to her bare breast, causing small cries of ecstasy to escape her, and she knew that the time had come, that the moment she had dreamed about would happen here and now on Kapiti.

His lips returned to hers, and as the kiss deepened on a rising tide of passion a tremor shook her, causing him to pause and stare into her eyes, his expression serious. 'You're frightened,' he accused quietly. 'You're terrified to—to make love.'

She nodded, then quavered, 'I suppose most girls are,

the—the first time.'

He was silent for several long moments before he said, 'The first time for us must be perfect. It'll be exactly as you want it to be, in a bed after our marriage, so we'll wait.'

'I'd like that.' A deep sigh escaped her, a sigh of gratitude.

Brent stood up and dragged her to her feet. 'We'll go back to the beach and fill in time by drawing plans in the sand.'

She was puzzled. 'Plans for what?'

'Plans for extending my apartment into a home for my bride. We'll need a nursery and probably a room for your sisters. I doubt that they'll leave us alone. Perhaps I'd be wise to buy two extra horses.'

'You'd be even wiser to curb your generosity,' she warned.

'Oh, I don't know. Their matchmaking tactics were so obvious they were really funny. Naturally, they'll take the credit for having arranged our engagement.'

Lana laughed. 'Naturally. I can see you're beginning to know them quite intimately, but really they do mean well.'

A few hours later they pulled and tugged at the dinghy until it was in a position to be attached to the launch's painter, and later, as the tide began to creep round the stern of the *Leisure*, they went on board and waited for it to float.

It was dusk when they arrived home, and as they approached the mainland shore they could see people coming down to the beach from the guest-house. Brent stared at the small crowd, then said, 'I think we'll have to face a reception committee. No doubt they've been worried about us and have been watching for our lights.' He dropped anchor, seized the painter and nudged the dinghy alongside.

Lana peered through the gathering darkness at the people gathered on the beach. 'Most of the staff appeared to be there as well as a number of guests, and good heavens, I can see the twins, and *Mother and Father*. Why should they be here?'

As he helped her into the dinghy he said, 'I have a suspicion there's been a general panic. We were to have been home in time to greet the senior citizens at five o'clock, remember? Everyone knows that boating accidents are all too common round New Zealand waters.'

When they reached the shallow water Brent lifted Lana from the small boat, and as he carried her to dry land Hilary's voice floated towards them, her agitation evident. 'Where on *earth* have you been? We were so *worried*, we were afraid something *awful* had happened!'

Eunice's voice echoed tearfully. 'Thank heavens you're safe.'

The next instant they were surrounded by staff, guests and family while Brent explained the problem of the tide. Eric introduced him to John Glenny, while Eunice, Hilary and the twins clustered round Lana. The twins, she noticed, were agog with excitement.

Raewyn said, 'You'd better know that Mum has blabbed to Eric. He knows who you are.'

Lana drew a nervous breath. 'He does?'

Bronwyn added, 'It was when we rang to ask you to book us in for the horses tomorrow. It was about six o'clock and Eric said you'd been expected home by four-thirty at the latest.'

Raewyn snatched the story from Bronwyn. 'When we told Mum she nearly had a fit. She rushed to the phone and rang back, wanting to know why you'd be so late. Then she got really wild because she thought Eric sounded very casual and unconcerned so she flew up in the air and blew her top. She told him who you really were.'

Bronwyn cut in, 'You should have heard her yell at him! She shouted that any fool could have seen who you were for himself. And then she bundled us all in the car and we came at once.'

Hilary said quickly, 'It gave him a shock, but I can tell you he's quite delighted. In fact we both are.'

Lana's eyes were full of anxiety. 'You're sure about that?'

'Of course. Surely you can understand there have been times when he's wondered about what happened to you. He's even admitted to me that the thought of you often nagged at him.'

Eunice spoke to Hilary. 'Do you think he had a guilt complex?'

Hilary nodded. 'To be honest, I think he realised he'd done something that would have upset Ingrid, yet he was unable to see what else he could have done because of his circumstances at the time.'

Lana turned to where Eric was standing beside Brent and John Glenny. She knew he was staring at her through the gloom and the next instant he had crossed the sand to give her a hug. 'You're so like Ingrid,' he whispered in her ear. 'I've been a blind idiot.'

'I'd love to have seen her,' Lana said wistfully.

'There's a photo you can have,' he admitted gruffly. 'Hilary thinks I've destroyed it, but now I know she'll forgive me for not having done so.'

Her eyes glowed. 'You've kept it hidden?'

'It's in a safe-deposit box at the bank with other odds and ends, things like the engagement and wedding rings I gave Ingrid, and the jewellery she'd inherited from her grandmother. It's all yours now.'

'Oh, thank you!' Further words failed her.

'When I left for England I didn't know what to do with those things until the bank manager suggested the deposit box. We'll get them out at the first opportunity.'

Brent joined them at that moment and seemed to take control of the situation by declaring to everyone that he had an announcement to make. He placed an arm about Lana's shoulders and said to the small crowd of people, 'Ladies and gentleman, this seems to be an appropriate moment to inform family and staff that Lana and I are to be married. Tonigth there'll be champagne on the house for everyone.'

Cheers rose, and in the babble of excitement several of the staff members reminded each other about bets. The twins began an animated discussion about being bridesmaids, and Lana found herself being kissed by everyone. Congratulations were poured upon Brent, who insisted upon kissing her blushing face before the whole crowd, and as they made their way up to the guest-house Lana's cup of happiness brimmed to the top and ran over.

Later, as she stood beside him on the moonlit veranda, she was gripped by a feeling of unreality. 'It all seems like a dream,' she whispered, gazing at the glittering pathway cast across the water by the moon's rays. 'I feel as though I'm walking along that silver road out there.'

He drew her closer to him. 'And what will you find on the other side? Why, the island, of course. Something that's solid and lasting, and as enduring as my love for you will always be.'

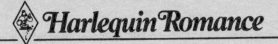

◆ *Harlequin Romance*

Coming Next Month

#3001   UNCONDITIONAL LOVE   Claudia Jameson
Coralie's new life in Salisbury is disturbed when Jake Samuels and
his son arrive and Jake offers her a decorating commission. Coralie
knows she can handle the arrogant Jake, but she's convinced
something's wrong in the Samuels household.

#3002   SEND IN THE CLOWN   Patricia Knoll
Kathryn, as her alter ego Katydid the Clown, had been adored by
thousands. But as Reid Darwin's temporary personal assistant life is
no circus. What did she have to do to win even a word of praise
from her toughest critic?

#3003   BITTERSWEET PURSUIT   Margaret Mayo
Charley isn't looking for romance—she just wants to find
her father. Yet thrown into constant contact with explorer
Braden Quest, who clearly opposes her presence on the jungle
expedition in Peru, Charley is aware of the intense feelings sparking
between them....

#3004   PARADISE FOR TWO   Betty Neels
Prudence doesn't regret giving up her own plans to accompany
her godmother to Holland. She finds her surroundings and her
hostess charming. However, she can't understand why the arrogant
Dr. Haso ter Brons Huizinga dislikes her—and tells herself she
doesn't care!

#3005   CROCODILE CREEK   Valerie Parv
Keri knows returning to the Champion cattle station can mean
trouble—yet her job as a ranger for Crocodile Task Force requires it.
Meeting Ben Champion again is a risk she must take—but it proves
more than she'd bargained for!

#3006   STILL TEMPTATION   Angela Wells
Verona is happy to accompany her young friend Katrina home to
Crete, but her excitement is dampened by Katrina's domineering
brother, Andreas, who expected a middle-aged chaperone, not an
attractive young woman. Suddenly Verona's anticipated holiday
turns into a battle of wills....

Available in September wherever paperback books are sold,
or through Harlequin Reader Service:

In the U.S.
901 Fuhrmann Blvd.
P.O. Box 1397
Buffalo, N.Y. 14240-1397

In Canada
P.O. Box 603
Fort Erie, Ontario
L2A 5X3

Harlequin American Romance®

Gull Cottage

The sun, the surf, the sand...

One relaxing month by the sea was all Zoe, Diana and Gracie ever expected from their four-week stay at Gull Cottage, the luxurious East Hampton mansion. They never thought that what they found at the beach would change their lives forever.

Join Zoe, Diana and Gracie for the summer of their lives. Don't miss the GULL COTTAGE trilogy in Harlequin American Romance: #301 CHARMED CIRCLE by Robin Francis (July 1989); #305 MOTHER KNOWS BEST by Barbara Bretton (August 1989); and #309 SAVING GRACE by Anne McAllister (September 1989).

GULL COTTAGE—because one month can be the start of forever...

GULLG-1

You'll flip . . . your pages won't!
Read paperbacks *hands-free* with

Book Mate · I

The perfect "mate" for all your romance paperbacks

Traveling · Vacationing · At Work · In Bed · Studying · Cooking · Eating

Perfect size for all standard paperbacks, this wonderful invention makes reading a pure pleasure! Ingenious design holds paperback books OPEN and FLAT so even wind can't ruffle pages – leaves your hands free to do other things. Reinforced, wipe-clean vinyl-covered holder flexes to let you turn pages without undoing the strap . . . supports paperbacks so well, they have the strength of hardcovers!

Pages turn WITHOUT opening the strap

SEE-THROUGH STRAP

Reinforced back stays flat

Built in bookmark

BOOK MARK

BACK COVER HOLDING STRIP

10 x 7¼ opened
Snaps closed for easy carrying, too

Available now. Send your name, address, and zip code, along with a check or money order for just $5.95 + 75¢ for postage & handling (for a total of $6.70) payable to Reader Service to:

Reader Service
Bookmate Offer
901 Fuhrmann Blvd
P.O. Box 1396
Buffalo, N.Y 14269-1396

Offer not available in Canada
*New York and Iowa residents add appropriate sales tax

BM-G